Mummy's Legs

KATE BINGHAM

A *Virago* Book

First published by Virago Press 1998

A CIP catalogue record for this book
is available from the British Library.

ISBN 1 86049 489 7

Typeset in Bembo by M Rules
Printed and bound in Great Britain by
CPD Wales, Ebbw Vale

Virago
A Division of
Little, Brown and Company (UK)
Brettenham House
Lancaster Place
London WC2E 7EN

Mummy's Legs

'Are we nearly there?' Sarah opened her eyes as the car changed down a gear. For a moment the road ahead seemed to vanish into hedgerow. She felt herself thrown hard into the side of the door, then swing back as they straightened out of the turn and once again their headlights beamed up the lane.

'I think so.'

'How nearly?'

'Not sure. Did you have a nice sleep?'

'Are we lost?' The silhouettes of trees, black against midnight blue, flashed past and a single electric light glowed faintly far away to their left.

'Probably,' said Harry, patting her leg cheerfully. 'Keep your eyes peeled for a sign to Oswold.'

A feeble yellowy grey cloud of light fanned out over the road about half a mile ahead of them. Farmhouse gables glimmered, then disappeared like ghosts. The light grew stronger.

'She will be all right, won't she?' said Sarah, thinking aloud. 'What's that?'

They rounded a bend. The road flooded with shining mist.

Harry dipped the headlights and the two cars passed in silence.

'Are you sure we're not lost?' They had taken the second left after the telephone box in accordance with Marion's instructions. Grasses poked through the tarmac in the middle of the lane and loose stones flicked the underneath of the car. They were driving very slowly now, Sarah on the lookout for hedgehogs and rabbits. Without warning, the tarmac gave way to dry mud, and a gate, decorated with a large white wooden cross, barred the track.

'Of course we aren't. Open it then.'

'But . . .' Sarah stared into the lit-up tufts of reedy grass. What if there were bulls on the other side?

'Go on.'

'You promise not to trick me?'

Harry promised. She got out and walked gingerly towards the gate. The catch lifted easily; it swung downhill away from the car, clanging like a gong as it crashed against a tree stump. A bird clapped free of the branches of an invisible tree close behind her and Sarah's heart pounded. The Rover slid forwards down the track and stopped a few feet clear of the gate, leaving her in eerie, red semi-darkness. She ran to the stump and quickly pushed the gate shut.

'Only one more,' said Harry as she threw herself back into the car. Sheep's eyes glittered in the headlights as they bumped slowly through the field.

On the far side of the second gate the track wound down through a field of slender barley. A lit window shone from between the trees below them, then vanished again as the car dipped over a ditch and passed through a copse. Leaves caressed the wing-mirrors like an intake of breath, and they saw the house.

Lights were on downstairs, throwing yellow squares onto the lawn, their sharp edges blurred by honeysuckle boughs. Hearing the engine, Marion and Jamie had risen from their seats round the kitchen table and stood frozen, it seemed, wine glasses in their hands. The Rover eased to a stop and Harry and Sarah sat in silence, spellbound and motionless, neither wanting to be first to speak or move. If only they could go on driving forever, she wished. Harry pushed his fingers up behind his glasses and rubbed his eyes.

The front door opened and Marion appeared, another block of yellow shining out behind her, stretching past her shadow into the mint and lavender bushes around the drive.

'Hello,' she said, rubbing her hands and peering into the darkness, 'we didn't expect to see you for hours. Has your father been speeding again?' Harry turned off the engine; they opened their doors and climbed out. Tinges of sunset burned a deep, corally red on the horizon, spreading and fading up into the dark blue sky. The scent of freshly cut nettles, of roses, jasmine, even the warm, sticky smell of animals in the next field hung in the air.

Marion gave Harry a hug and then walked round the back of the car to greet Sarah. 'How are you, pet? Has it been a very long day?' She kissed her forehead. An earring brushed against Sarah's cheek. It tickled. Marion always wore dangly earrings.

Jamie came out of the house and shook hands with Harry.

'No trouble finding us, then? I'm afraid Marion is famous for giving hopelessly inaccurate directions.'

'Oh no, it couldn't have been easier,' Harry beamed at them, 'though Sarah was sure I'd gone wrong. I usually do.'

'Well *you* didn't have to open the gates, did you!'

'You could have driven if you'd wanted—'

'Don't tease me,' she said, pretending to kick her father. Jamie opened the boot and lifted out their suitcases easily.

'What a place!' Harry looked round at the black outlines of outbuildings, then up at the stars. 'How long is it now?'

'Three months.'

'I wish I'd come sooner.' They walked indoors.

Ollie raced out into the hall to meet them, overshooting in a frenzy of enthusiasm. He skittered uncontrollably on the tiles, regained his balance and bounded back, circling Sarah, wagging his tail and jumping up to lick her nose.

'Ollie, love, come here!' Marion patted her knees and, after a moment's hesitation, the spaniel abandoned his prey. 'Now calm down, or you'll frighten Sarah and she won't want to be your friend.' He gazed up at his mistress and licked her hands. Marion had the same soft, almost-not-there smile as her cousin, Sarah's mum. She had the same brown eyes too but her hair was dark and wavy and she was taller and not so thin. She looked questioningly at Sarah.

'Are you hungry, or do you want to go straight up?' They were in the kitchen. A jug of grass flowers, cow-parsley and mint and a half-finished bottle of red wine stood at the near end of a vast kitchen table. A sprinkling of tiny, white cow-parsley flowers lay at the base of the jug like a feeble shadow, or a halo, and flies corkscrewed under the light as if in imitation of the dog. The two men hesitated, and for a moment buzzing was all that could be heard.

'I think I'll go to bed, if that's all right,' said Sarah.

'Of course it is, pet! I bet you're exhausted. Come on then.'

Jamie said good night and Harry promised to be up in a minute.

'Which is your case, my love?'

Sarah pointed and shyly followed her upstairs. They hadn't seen each other much in the last few years, except at Christmas.

The hall ran along almost the whole length of the back of the house, its cobwebby white walls indiscriminately lined with what seemed to Sarah like the contents of an old junk shop: bookcases which sagged with warped and musty out-of-print hardbacks, a coat-stand, moth-eaten shooting caps on hat pegs, dark Victorian oils, a row of old framed photographs. Sarah stopped to look at them more closely.

'That's Pip, Jamie's grandmother's dog,' said Marion, pointing at a picture of a small black and white spotted terrier, posed grandly on a croquet lawn in front of a large country house. 'And that's where they lived. This way.' Wicker baskets, scythes and ragged bunches of dried flowers hung from the beams on rusting nails.

A dimly lit, narrow corridor stretched right and left at the top of the stairs, Marion turned right and pushed open a door with a flourish. 'Do you like it?'

There were three beds in the room, which smelled of mice and heated-up dust. The thinly carpeted floor sloped crookedly towards a single window. Antique blue wallpaper hung from the ceiling in yellowed curls. Bare electrical wires were all that prevented the light switch from falling out of its crumbling plaster nook in the wall. Marion turned back the cover of the furthest bed and unzipped Sarah's bag, rummaging through for a nightie.

'I can do that.'

She hesitated. 'Of course you can, love. I'm sorry. Didn't mean to be nosy.' She stepped back and waited as Sarah tipped the contents of her case onto one of the spare beds and quickly picked out her pyjamas. 'Where's the bathroom?'

'At the end on the left—'

'Thanks.' Sarah disappeared.

'The light switch is outside . . .'

Her father came in to tuck her up. 'Is this OK, cherub?' he asked, bending over to stroke her hair.

Sarah nodded. 'How long are you staying?'

'I ought to get back tomorrow, but I'll try and come for a weekend soon. Marion will look after you.'

'It's not the same.'

'I know,' he kissed her eyelids, then straightened up. 'It's the best we can do.'

He pulled the door to and went downstairs, the corridor creaking with every step. His leather shoes slapped on the tiles in the hall. The latch clicked and the kitchen door banged shut. Adult voices drifted up through the floorboards, hard to make out at first. Sarah lay quietly and listened.

'So how is she?'

'OK. They're keeping her in for surveillance. She'll be released in a day or two, stupid girl.' It was her father; he sounded very tired.

'Have a drink,' said Jamie.

'Thanks. I need one.'

'How was the drive?'

'Oh, fine. Unreal. Sarah was quiet – as you'd expect, I suppose. She's been terribly brave, almost matter-of-fact about it.'

'Poor thing.'

'Does she understand?'

'Oh, perfectly. If anyone's in the dark it's me. I should never have moved out.'

'No one's blaming you,' said Jamie.

'I am. I was there, she actually called me round. I should have known. I should have stayed – kept an eye on her.'

'She's not a child—'

'She just behaves like one,' Marion muttered bitterly, interrupting. 'This is classic emotional blackmail. Foot-stamping! I grew up with her, remember. I've seen it before. I know you feel responsible, Harry – of course you do, it's only natural – but let it go! Just let it go. It's Catherine's fault, not yours.'

There was a heavy pause, broken by the sound of Ollie, skidding and scampering across the floor. He must have frightened himself: he barked once, curtly.

'Ollie shut up,' Jamie growled back. 'What exactly did the doctors say?'

'Nothing much. She'll make a full recovery but, well, she took all sorts of stuff – quite a cocktail – so they need to keep her in to make sure there aren't going to be any unexpected side-effects. I'm supposed to have a word with our GP, put him on the alert. The other question is,' he groaned, 'whether I should move back in – for a month or so.'

'Has she been working?'

'God knows. She stays in bed a lot, reads all the papers from cover to cover, writes the odd review. Apart from that she does what she wants.'

'As usual,' said Marion.

Jamie cleared his throat. 'Moving in might make matters worse—'

'But at least I'd be there to stop her trying again.'

'Ollie . . . ! How have you been getting on?'

'Hard to say. She's been so worried about David – ever since Christmas, she seems to have forgotten me. For a while I was actually relieved. Which makes me feel worse now, of course.'

'Do you want to move in again?'

Harry shrugged.

'If you go back,' said Marion, 'she'll only think her melo-dramatics have succeeded.'

'Come on now, love. That's a bit harsh, isn't it?' said Jamie.

'We all have to learn how to cope with losing the things we love.' Marion insisted. 'Even Catherine.' They paused.

'But what if she does it again? What if next time she wakes up and doesn't bother calling the Samaritans?'

'Then she's more of a bloody fool than I thought.' Marion hesitated, then said more softly, 'I don't know. Was it a serious attempt?'

'What does the doctor think?' asked Jamie.

'I haven't asked. I'll talk to him when they let her out.' There was a long silence. 'Anyway, thank you both for being here.'

'Come on, Harry. That's what families are for.'

Another pause. 'Hey, it's a stunning place you've got your-
selves here.'

'Wait until you see it in daylight.'

'Mmm. Actually, I'm pretty exhausted. Mind if I go to
bed?' Chairs scraped back from the table as they stood up and
cleared away their glasses.

I go by bus, sitting on the upper deck right at the front, by the window, the very best seat. Branches clatter against the roof as we speed down Brompton Road towards an amber traffic light and I squeeze the handrail like a roller-coaster rider. It is a beautiful day, warm already with thin white clouds that drift up from the skyline, sauntering towards the sun only to evaporate into trails of haze. Aeroplane tracks. Thick shadows blot the glare of the pavements and the roads are dappled with the silhouettes of plane trees. There is hardly anyone about, the bus is empty. I am self-consciously contented, like a holiday-maker; guilty as a truant and utterly without remorse. Fresh air rushes through the open window and the noise is pure exhilaration. White lines seem to vanish beneath the front of the bus at dizzying speed and the brakes squeal vivaciously as we swoop to a perfect, last-minute stop.

At the florist's I choose three bunches of yellow lilies and an expensive card from their exclusive selection. The flowers are wrapped in beautiful, clear, scratch-free plastic foil, and a yellow ribbon to match is fastened around their stems. As I write in the card with a borrowed pen, the shop assistant opens his scissors and runs each end of the ribbon, swiftly, between his

thumb and the blade, making two cascades of shiny curls.
These he twists into an elaborate bow, asking, as if to prove
that he is competent to do more than one thing at a time, 'Are
they for someone special?'

My mother was born the day the Allies bombed Nagasaki.
Ma, my grandmother, threw a party with bread and jam, and
jelly, and little boys and girls from other Methodist,
Conservative-voting families in York all playing hunt-the-
thimble together in their smartest Sunday clothes.

I nod at him. 'Mum. She's fifty today.'

'Be careful of the stamens.' The shop assistant brushes one
of the hammer-heads gently and shows his finger coated in
paprika. 'The pollen stains.' He passes me the flowers and we
say goodbye; as I leave the shop, stepping into the sunshine
like a bride emerging from the church, he is already wiping
his finger carefully with a piece of tissue.

She lives in the house where I grew up, on a peaceful, cherry-
lined street in South Kensington bought in the seventies, so the
story goes, from a retired prostitute. Tall and rather stately, it
has a deep, high-ceilinged, south-facing ground-floor room
which someone from Habitat once wanted to use as a catalogue set. A new conservatory lined with books, geraniums
and hardy ferns leads off to one side above the kitchen.
Redecorated when I went to university, this is the sort of
room that passers-by look in on and envy. I envy it too, knowing I will never be able to afford a place as grand or as elegant.
And even if I could, that I will never have friends as grand or
elegant to fill it with – the columnists and Channel Four pro-
fessors she gets round for after-work drinks in the summer.

A shiny, black Bechstein grand stands in the window, on felt-based wooden castors so as not to make holes in the maple-wood floor. It was bought when I was eight or nine, according to Marion, to stop Dad trying to move us into a smaller house. Mum can pick out one or two carols and hymns, but doesn't really like to play because, she says, it makes her sad.

I rest the lilies against the front door step and rummage through my bag for the keys which, though I moved out more than a year ago, I still carry with me everywhere. I sort through the post, feeling a spark of the old excitement. When I was a child everything about the post excited me. The way you couldn't be sure exactly when it would arrive and had to listen out for the postman during breakfast but not let anyone see that that was what you were doing because a watched kettle never boils. The rattle of the letterbox and the slap of the paper on the doormat and the way you could tell how much there was by measuring the gap between them. How different kinds of letter had distinguishable sounds. Bills from the newsagent's, for instance, were usually so light they would glide like paper aeroplanes, delicately stroking the bristles of the mat as they landed. I was a connoisseur of paper-fall. I loved the secrecy of envelopes, and their vulnerability. The fact that people trusted the Post Office to deliver them unopened. I loved the thought that something unexpected, from anyone, anywhere in the whole wide world, might already be on its way; every morning but Sunday, the possibility that a letter might come to change your life.

Then, one summer when I was ten, a letter like that did come. It was addressed to me and started, 'Please don't show

this letter to anyone else.' I took it outside to read because I
could tell it would make me cry and I didn't want the others
to see and get curious. After I had finished reading it and finished crying, not so much because of what it said as because
I very much loved the person who had written it and missed
them badly, I folded it up and hid it in the lining of my suitcase. And, without necessarily meaning to, I have carried it
with me ever since. The suitcase has lasted better than the letter, whose envelope is worn to cotton at the edges and greasy
with sun-tan lotion, but I like the thought of it there, and I
like the thought that Ben might, just might, find it by accident
this weekend, and read it.

'I hope he isn't going to break your heart,' says Mum, when
he first starts phoning me at home.

'He's just a friend,' I murmur, taking the receiver and waving her into the bathroom. According to seismologists, even
London suffers a number of small earthquakes each year, and
perhaps this is why the door will no longer pull completely
shut. It jars and shudders against the frame and in the background I can hear coat hangers lightly scraping the clothes
rail. The bath runs. I talk to Ben in short, embarrassed flour-
ishes and make an arrangement. Mum reappears, as if by
chance, the moment he clicks off.

'Well,' she continues, tiptoeing back across the carpet in
stockinged feet with a half-folded sweater under her arm and
a look of recently satisfied curiosity on her face, 'you may
think he's just a friend but I'm telling you it won't stay like
that for long.'

'How do you know?' I colour.

She taps her nose smugly and grins. 'Be careful. I'm not saying *he* is, but remember most of them are bastards.'

It is the week before Christmas and traffic-policemen have been drafted in to guard the pedestrians on Oxford Street. Piccadilly is fogged with car exhaust. Claxons ricochet down Burlington Arcade and shopping bags collide head-on in the throng. The Royal Academy courtyard seems a frozen, grey oasis of calm by comparison. Only the pigeons move, fluttering and feinting for crumbs amongst the cigarette ends.

Ben is standing by the steps with his hands in his pockets and his shoulders hunched against the cold, watching me. The tube was delayed by signal failure at Barons Court and I have kept him waiting. I am about to burst with apologies but I know I mustn't be seen to run or quicken my pace. I pretend to be looking at something else; windows and parked cars flicker slowly through the corners of my field of vision until, at last, I am standing next to him, wondering how to say hello. Sometimes really acute self-consciousness can have a liberating effect. I do not touch him, even with the rucked-up sleeve of my coat, and we both know why. We buy our tickets and wander up to the galleries, peeling off sweaters and extra sweaters as we go. My shoulder-bag vanishes beneath a curtain of clothes and suddenly I am almost twice as wide as usual, brushing through doorways and crashing into people as I turn to check he's still there. He smiles at me and I look away.

I go round room one too fast, lapping him on the second wall, and stand there, silently, at his shoulder. The models are *jolie-laid*, their faces strongly defined, already, by Schiele's characteristic black and green outlines. Together we drift through to the later work and now not even the canvasses are a safe place for me to keep my eyes. The walls are lined with half-naked women, sitting, standing, crouching, stretching, curled up masturbating on the studio floor and, however objectively I argue to myself that nakedness and the free expression of sexuality in art are Good and Not Embarrassing, there is still something undeniably ugly and familiar about their unrepentant heavy white bodies. It feels as though he has painted in my muscles and bruises, dimples and folds with almost iconoclastic vigour and I don't like Ben examining them.

Shouting breaks the reverent atmosphere, and a troupe of gallery attendants rushes through to the next-door room. A tramp has got in and fallen over, drunk, on the polished parquet, face to face with an elaborate iron vent. He is shouting for air so the attendants pick him up and take him outside. Ben stands in the corner scribbling on his free exhibition guide.

'Making notes?' I whisper.

'Sort of.' He presses it secretively to his chest. 'Have you had enough?'

In the courtyard it has started to get dark. The sky is gradually turning an icy twilight blue. The pigeons have flown away. We could go home now, separate on the chilly pavement with a casual goodbye. Another whole week, another whole term could pass. Instead we walk to Piccadilly Circus. Cordings has knocked twenty per cent off the price of its cashmere coats. Small crowds gawp in at Fortnum and Mason's lavish mechanised window display.

Wild at Heart is showing at the MGM. We find our seats as the trailers finish and the curtains swish shut, pointlessly. The

lights dip up. The carpet is streaked with little puffy clouds of
popcorn. Ben and I wait formally in our adjacent chairs.
When the lights go out again we shuffle, trying to get comfortable. His elbow nudges the arm-rest.

When the struck match flares I glance across at him and see
the flame projected back off the screen, ducking and swallowing in his eye. The Nic Cage character has just been
released from prison and he and Laura Dern make love over
and over in a sequence of increasingly seedy motels. I sit very
still and stare straight ahead. After this, I think, I will never be
able to look at him again without blushing.

Hanging from the door to the kitchen is a necklace of water-
melon pips and nut-shells, collected and dried for a school
project when I was in the infants. This means the burglar
alarm is on, though I know she's in – her BMW is parked
outside. Leaving it on makes her feel safer. The neighbours
have lined their windows with iron bars and pull-across
accordion grilles. At least my mother's defences are invisible.

As the front door swings shut the building shudders into
absolute quietness. The narrow, sunless hall is cool like a
cathedral cloister and smells of make-up, that possibly unique
combination of Elizabeth Arden and Lancôme which she
wears every day. The scent is a second presence in the house,
the smell of homesickness just before it hits you. The smell of
a ghost.

Upstairs, in the study, the blinds are down and a red light
flashes on and off, quickly, on the answer-machine. Book-
towers and paper-mounds cover the floor and desk. Last year
her Olive Schreiner biography almost won the Whitbread

and now she's trying to go one better with Sarah Grand. She
has been secretly frantic, writing up research in fits and starts
all summer. Her laptop sits on the armchair in a pool of sunlight. Cashmere sweaters lean against the back of the sofa on
a towel, drying next to the radiator. The heat is stifling. I
wonder if she's still asleep and, if so, whether to wake her. I
wonder how long the lilies will last out of water.

In the kitchen I pull the blinds, squinting up through the
sudden brightness deep into the branches of a cherry tree. For
one week at the beginning of April every year, this street is the
prettiest in London, an avenue of pink and white blossom. The
gutters float with petals. The pavements are littered with small
branches broken off by enthusiasts and, found too cumber-
some, abandoned, their frilly white clusters yellowing already,
like warm snow. In June, wisteria cascades from the wrought-
iron balconies of the house next door. Now though, the trees
and creepers are deep and palpy with leaves. The cars parked
nose to nose like a second, inner, avenue are dappled. From
between *Poor Cook* and *Soup, Beautiful Soup*, I shuffle out a
folded, fading, falling-to-pieces 1967 edition of *Woman's Own*.

Covered with grease-spots and raw egg varnish, its pages
have long lost their original flexibility and need to be folded
the exact same way every time, like an ancient map, so that
whenever anyone wants the recipe for chocolate devil's food
cake the first thing their eyes will fall upon is an article enti-
tled 'Sex Problems Solved'. Today, for the very first time, I
read this article. Then I turn over the page (the paper creaks)
and find the recipe. Having taken an envelope out of the bin
in the study, and a pencil from my mother's pencil jar, I write
a list of ingredients.

Halfway through this preliminary, which I perform as quietly as possible, she wakes up. 'Sarah, is that you?' she calls out, slurring sleepfully. I put down the caster sugar, open the kitchen door, pick up the lilies from the landing table, tiptoe upstairs and venture into her bedroom, rustling.

'Happy Birthday, Mum. Did I wake you?'

'Not really,' she yawns. 'What time is it?'

I look at my watch, getting used to the darkness slowly, and guess eleven.

'Turn on the light. I've got something to show you.'

'What is it? Flowers? I can smell them.'

'Lilies.'

'Funeral flowers.'

'Mum . . .'

Now I can see her reach out a hand and fumble for the light switch. For an instant everything goes bright and the lilies gleam. I see her short, blonde hair fanned out on the pillow behind, her dark eyes flicker. Then she turns it off again, saying flatly, 'Very nice. Yellow.'

'I'll go and put them in some water, shall I?' I reply, as if I have swallowed some of the electric light. 'Do you want coffee?'

She sighs. 'I'll make it. If you could just put the kettle on.'

'Everything gives you cancer or makes you sterile,' I used to say when grown-ups told me not to eat sweets or watch so much TV. Nowadays they speak of positive and negative effects. The negative effect of living on your own is creeping intolerance. People lose the habit of compromise, forget what it's like to have their whims and peculiarities questioned.

It starts off slowly, like an invisible disease, when solitude is a new and joyful revelation of independence: the freedom to sing along with Sinatra on Radio Two during breakfast without having anyone to laugh at you, to sleep with the bedroom window shut on cold winter nights. But, as the illness establishes itself, these autonomies, once a source of self-expression and delight, harden into something else. What used to be regarded as a privilege becomes a human right. Civil liberty is running three saucers through the dishwasher, leaving the bathroom light on day and night. An invitation to the theatre is interpreted as an attack upon free will. As if resentful of the hard-earned freedom to eat home-delivered pizza for dinner every night of the week, lovers, relatives and close friends seem intent upon destroying the victim's happy equilibrium.

My mother drifts into the kitchen wearing her dressing gown and creases her eyes at the daylight. Her silver-blonde curls are squashed against the back of her head where she has been lying on them. She looks at the lilies, which I have arranged in the blue glass vase I gave her for a birthday several years ago, and sees, I imagine, something yellow that smells, cluttering up her nice white wall. If she had wanted a yellow wall she would have had it painted that colour; if she had wanted flowers for her birthday she would have phoned up Interflora and ordered them by American Express herself.

Then she surprises me. She walks up to the lilies, really close, and breathes in deeply. She lifts her head and looks out of the kitchen window up into the street and says, 'What an amazing smell. They're beautiful. Thank you.'

It wins me, instantly. 'That's OK, Mum. Look, I got you a card as well.'

She opens the envelope and reads the message inside. 'Are you going to make me a birthday cake then?'

'Yes,' I say, as gently as possible, filled with tenderness. 'I'm just working out what ingredients to buy.'

'Has the kettle boiled?'

'It has.'

'Move over then and let me make myself a cup of coffee.'

She turns in from the window and I look at her face. Along with traces of yesterday's mascara, her cheeks are slashed with pollen.

She seems quite cheerful, considering it's her fiftieth, standing there by the window with her face sucked in as I dab at the pollen with a piece of damp kitchen roll, impatiently asking me if it's gone yet, like a child enjoying the attention. The kettle is boiled a second time; I write cooking chocolate on the list. A moment later, though, I hear a bottle top spin and whisky is added to the ritual of powders – coffee, sugar, milk – and my optimism vanishes. It is just as if the sun had disappeared behind a thick black cloud.

She watches me noticing and says, 'I don't drink much, you know, only occasionally. This is the only drop I've had for days. Days! To help me through my birthday . . .'

'Why? What's happened?'

She stirs the froth two revolutions, more vigorously than with her fragile, dishevelled look she would seem capable of. 'Apart from a call from David last night, nothing's *happened*. Nothing ever *happens*.'

'David? That's nice. What did he want?'

'I don't know. What do men ever want? If I knew that do you think I would be like this?' In silence we both look down at her purple and white checked cotton nightie. 'He asked me out for lunch.'

'That's nice,' I say again, brightly. 'When?'

'Today. I wish I knew what the bastard was up to.'

'What do you mean?'

She shrugs, grumpily, and scrunches her hair. 'Well, he must be up to something, or why would he have called?'

'To say happy birthday? He wants to take you out. What's wrong with that?'

'Come off it, Sarah!' Sometimes she worries that every-thing she has ever told me about 'the way things work' will have been to no avail. 'Your ex-lover phones up on your birthday and asks to take you out! He's after something, I'll bet you a hundred pounds.'

'Are you going then?'

'Where?'

'Out to lunch.'

'Oh that – yes.' She sucks her coffee spoon. 'What time is it? I'd better get ready.' When Mum sees David she never seems to enjoy herself. She books an appointment with the hairdresser in Bond Street the afternoon before, to give her-self time to make alterations if there's a disaster, and spends at least an hour choosing what to wear and putting on her face. She goes out of her way to look as glamorous as possible.

They drink a lot and eat, I suspect, very little. Like most fifty-somethings, they are watching their weight. His back has got worse and his bald patch larger; he is getting old. By contrast, she seems younger and younger every time they meet, and flirts in inverse proportion to how good a time she's having, to how full the bottle is. She usually lets him pay and always declines his last sly, sheepish invitation. This is the focus of her self-respect, but self-respect isn't always enough. She comes home lonely and depressed. She doesn't want to grow old on her own. Her friends assume it's only a matter of time before they get back together again.

'Don't you want any breakfast?'

'No thanks. I feel a bit sick to tell the truth.' A cluster of dirty white bubbles still sails gently round the perimeter of her coffee cup as she carries it out of the kitchen.

I follow her up into the bathroom, only to back out again as I realise she's on the loo.

'It's OK,' she mutters, 'you don't have to go.' There is a short, uncomfortable silence.

'So where's he taking you?' I hover awkwardly in the door-way.

'Don't know. He says he's going to pick me up.'

'And what are you going to wear?'

'Not sure. Is it hot?' She flushes the chain and the house springs to life as water courses wildly through invisible pipes.

'Incredibly hot.' I begin to rummage through her clothes, which hang from a long steel tube suspended between the boiler and the wall. When I was younger they used to be crammed together as tight as a rail in a charity shop, but there's plenty of room now. Her winter suits are in a spare room upstairs, packed away into moth-proof dustbin liners.

'Maybe I'll wear my white minidress – that'll give him a shock. And paint my nails bright red. What do you think?'

'Maybe,' I say. 'You don't need anything from the shops, do
you?'

'No.'

'I'll see you in a minute, then.' I close the door, leaving her
to her mirror, and run downstairs.

Marion woke early, as she did every morning, and lay for a while on her back, staring up at the cracks in the ceiling and listening to the tap of the blind on the window frame. It seemed amazing that she could still remember a time when peaceful, solitary moments like this had used to flood her with an almost religious sense of thankfulness – for the start of a brand-new day, for what she had to look forward to. In her childhood, had it been? Or the early days of her marriage?

Birds were singing outside and a fly knocked blindly into the light-shade. Next to her, his broad back curled towards the fireplace, Jamie slept peacefully. And now there was a child in the house, after all. Not hers, but flesh and blood all the same. Marion wondered if Sarah was awake. Harry still slept. She could hear his deep, apparently contented snores through the wall. Had he kept that up all night? She remembered sniggering about it with Catherine on a girls' night out, just after the two of them had first moved in together, but the noise didn't bother her. It was a relief to have other people in the house. They had fallen in love with it at first sight, though right from the start she had said it was too big.

'People will come for long weekends, we won't be able to get rid of them,' Jamie had argued. 'We'll fill it. And what we can't fill we'll simply forget about.'

But Harry and Sarah were practically their first guests, not counting Jamie's mother and father, and it had been three months.

She crawled out from beneath the covers and threw on yesterday's jeans, a sweatshirt and a pair of trainers. Jamie stretched out an arm to feel her absence and rolled sleepily into the space, folding back the covers. He always woke too hot, grizzled with beard.

'Do you want a cup of tea?'

'No thanks.' He cleared his throat. 'Better get up too.'

Marion tried to ignore her disappointment. 'See you in a minute, then.'

She left the room, hesitating outside Sarah's door on her way to the loo. The telltale floorboards creaked beneath their threadbare red carpet.

'Shake out all those spiders.'

'And mice!'

Sarah tipped the wellington boot upside down, bashing its toe with the heel of her hand. The top of the boot had indeed been nibbled by a mouse or possibly, to guess from the size of the teeth-marks, a rat. Squinting into its impenetrable rubbery darkness, then leaning back against Harry for support, she plunged her foot inside, hobbled once or twice and pulled a face.

'It's too small.'

Marion was puzzled. 'Are you sure?'

'Have you got any more?'

'No, pet.' Almost tenderly she picked up the other boot and examined its sole. 'This is all.'

'Never mind,' said Jamie, stamping the dry mud from his boots just outside the door. 'We haven't had much rain lately. She'll be fine in shoes.'

Crestfallen, Sarah appealed to her father.

'We'll carry you over the sticky bits,' he promised. They strolled out into the yard where the cars were parked.

'Of course there's a lot of work to be done . . .' Jamie was saying.

Harry interrupted him. 'Wow!'

Separated from the rest of the garden by an L-shaped, flowering dry-stone wall, the yard was a wilderness of grasses, lavender, mint and nettles, grown up between the cobbles over years of neglect. The track they had driven along the night before swung round the outside of the yard and up a gentle hill beside the house where, vanishing into the grass, it ended at a rusty five-bar gate.

'It's magical.'

Jamie beamed with delight. 'I'm glad you like it. We're besotted, of course, but we all have our doubts. When it rains for days on end—'

'And we get nostalgic for shopping centres, traffic jams and the cinema,' Marion added lightly, smiling a private, radiant smile. Harry looked away. His shoes were already damp with dew and peppered with tiny purplish grass seeds.

'Where to now?' he said at last, breaking the silence.

'Let's play Orpheus and Euridice,' suggested Marion.

'What?' Harry glanced at Jamie, who simply shrugged.

'We walk up there,' she pointed to the ridge-line on the far side of the valley, 'and no one's to look back before we get to the top.'

'Or what?' asked Sarah, coming to life.

'Or they have to do the washing-up.'

'No problem! Come on, Dad, I'll race you.' Sarah turned her back on the house and set off jauntily.

One by one the others followed her, down to the stream, across the footbridge, through the bog at the bottom of the opposite field, past cows, and up into the second field. Barley grew on one side of the hedge, ground-peas on the other.

'It's all so green,' said Harry, stopping to catch his breath. Sarah had run on ahead, he could see her just about to reach the road now, and he was beginning to feel uncomfortable without her chatter for company. 'This is one of my favourite times of year. Is that the barley I can smell?'

'Mmm.' Marion paused. She had also stopped, a little way behind him, and was peering scientifically into the bramble hedge. 'Does Sarah remember Toby, do you think?' she asked, almost casually.

'Of course she does.' Harry turned to face her. He had been waiting for this.

'I mean, does she ever talk about him?'

'No-o. It's not . . .' He fumbled for the right way to put it, then lost his train of thought. 'It's not the sort of thing she *would* talk about.'

'I keep thinking about how sweet they were together, as toddlers. Really sweet – sharing their toys and looking after each other, not like most kids. We were all so proud of them for that. Do you remember?'

'Yes.'

She pulled at a blade of grass, shredding the flower-head between her fingernails, waiting. If only she could find some-one who would talk to her about Toby. It was as if people were frightened of him. They wanted to forget, they assumed she wanted to forget, they didn't want to have to see her cry, remembering. 'What happy days!'

'It was fun,' he said, smiling weakly. 'Shall we catch up with the others?'

'Looks like Dad'll be washing up lunch!' Jamie strode eas-ily onto the lane, filled his huge lungs with the scented air and smiled at Sarah.

She nodded. They gazed down the field, past Harry and Marion, and across the valley to where the farmhouse seemed to nestle, surrounded by outbuildings and trees. More fields rose serenely behind it, rolling off in a patchwork to the near horizon.

It was time for Harry to go. They had tramped the eighteen-acre field and walked in the garden, listened to Jamie's plans for a vegetable patch and tried the swing. They had ventured blindly into overgrown, collapsing out-buildings and jumped half out of their skins as wood-pigeon abandoned their roosts on unclaimed rafters. In the principal barn they had seen an owl. Lunch had been a picnic on the lawn in front of the house, with plates and glasses passed out through an open window. Marion had insisted on doing the washing-up. One meal gave way to the next, a brief round of croquet amongst the molehills marking a boundary of sorts between. Piled with cakes, the breadboard had attracted the attention of several insect species but, flapping ceaselessly against the buddleia, the butterflies had refused to be lured onto their sugary fingers.

Slowly the afternoon light thickened. Slouching on tattered Turkish rugs, the adults chatted easily, as if the Catherines and Tobys of their imagination had simply stepped out for a walk together and were due back later. They cherished their last few moments of stolen idleness, Sarah's far-away babble indistinguishable from the chorus of birds. A pink sun disappeared behind the cow shed. The air grew cool, dew fell. Marion stood up.

'Are you sure you won't stay for supper?'

'No, I've got an early start in the morning.'

'A drink, then?'

Harry rubbed his eyes and shook his head regretfully.

Sarah rode with him as far as the second gate, waving him out of sight as the Rover accelerated up-hill. Loose gravel scattered in its wake and a trail of dust drifted lazily into the hedgerows. Intently, she watched a blade of grass, a full handspan taller than its neighbours in the middle of the track, waver as the tarmac relinquished the last of its heat. All of a sudden, she realised, it was nearly dark.

Sarah doesn't recall the first time she met David Finch, though she would have thought that something sharp and bright in her mother's expression at the moment of introduction might have stuck a bookmark in her memory. She supposes she must have been a baby, or a very young child, and that his tanned face and blond side-parting were simply added, along with grandparents, family car and front door, to the category of Things I Know without her noticing. It seems strange only with hindsight that he was always there and, even then, not very strange. After all, there was no love lost between her parents – how they had ever managed to agree a time and place to get married is a private family mystery. They argued, sometimes violently, about a variety of trivial matters and were indefatigably opposed on every controversial issue of the day. Her mother used to boast at dinner parties that she knew, the moment they signed the register, she had made a terrible mistake. To keep up, her father would exaggerate the disappointments of their honeymoon in Provence. Absence of marital affection topped their daughter's lengthening list of Things I Understand. She wishes they could be a normal family, but there is nothing to be done.

David Finch is a poet, with several well-reviewed collections to his name. He is very tall and strong-looking, like
Harry but, Sarah agrees disloyally, more handsome. He wears
patterned shirts and a fading denim jacket, with a scratchy
dog-tooth overcoat on top in winter. All Harry's clothes are
navy blue because Catherine once said it was the only colour
that didn't make him look unwell. David's hair is grainy like
sand and he washes it every day. Sometimes Sarah gets to
watch him putting his contact lenses in.

In spite of having inherited land and property, he is poor.
So poor he had to sell the manor – leaving his elderly mother
to the mercies of the local nursing home – and then, year by
year, the fields as well. He has no money sense, which is one
of the reasons why women like Catherine find him so attrac-
tive. Some would say he has cultivated an air of vulnerability
with exactly this end in mind, but who is Sarah to judge? All
she knows is that his twice-weekly visits are preceded by a
gradual build-up of anxious excitement which infects the
whole house.

'Sarah,' Catherine would call.

Sarah takes the stairs two steps at a time, thunders through
the study and swings round the bathroom door. 'Yes?'

'Where's your father?'

'Gardening.'

Catherine blinks beyond her heavy-lashed reflection and
pulls a face. 'Come here.' She takes a brush and positions her
daughter in front of the mirror. Sarah tenses her neck against
the downstroke as the knots unpull, her hair flying out in a
crackling, static cone which her mother smoothes, her soft,
empty hand alternating with the unkind brush. 'Be a good

girl and tidy up for me downstairs. He'll be here soon and I
haven't finished putting on my face. And if the doorbell rings
don't answer it.'

Sarah breathes in her mother's scent and is happy. She
knows he'll be late. He lives in Kentish Town and travels
everywhere by bus because, says Catherine, he's scared to
drive and doesn't like the dirt in the Underground. He is
the only adult Sarah can think of who doesn't have a car.
The doorbell will go, her mother will hurry downstairs to
let him in and suddenly – and this is why Sarah willingly
runs to change her dress and tidy away her toys from the
drawing-room floor – she is happy. Everything turns all
right.

There is a thick, fumbling silence in the hall, then the click
of Catherine's heel as she steps from the door mat. She leads
him down, offering biscuits and coffee interspersed with light
apologies for the state of the house, the garden (this is code for
him to look through the back window and see Harry, pulling
up weeds in the sunshine) and he grins shyly at everything he
sees. Sarah offers to show him a story she has written for
school and, as she races to her room to find it, David and
Catherine kiss in the kitchen.

'Hello.'

The lovers spring apart and laugh awkwardly as Harry
squeezes past to get to the sink; his hands are filthy, a black
slug curls beneath each fingernail.

'Afternoon,' grins David. 'How's the garden?'

'Full of stones.' Harry plasters muddy palm-prints all over
the shining aluminium taps. 'How's my wife?'

David looks Catherine up and down as if considering this

question. Catherine nervously spoons Nescafé into a mug. Sarah crashes into the scene and thrusts her exercise book into David's hands. 'Can we go now, Dad?'

'In a minute.'

'Where are you off to?' asks David.

'They're going to Fulham Road to see a film, and then out for a hamburger,' says Catherine, holding her breath.

'Lucky you,' says David to Sarah.

'Do you want to come too?'

He looks from the daughter to the husband, as if tempted.

'No, Sarah, David's got a lot of work to do.'

'I'd love to,' he mutters simultaneously, 'but—'

'Another time, maybe,' says Harry, rescuing the situation. He rinses off the last of the soap and shakes his hands dry. Sarah is shunted out of the kitchen. The lovers half relax. In the hall Sarah will be sitting on the top stair waiting for her father. They will hear money and keys jangling as he runs down to her. They will chorus goodbye as the front door opens and the house sucks in. It is a bright, windy Saturday afternoon. Weekends have been like this for as long as any of them can remember.

Then the door blows shut and they are alone in the shuddering house. Catherine looks at the floor. 'It's a shame you didn't come a bit sooner,' she says mildly. 'Sarah was really excited about showing you her story.' *And you still haven't read my piece in the* TLS.

David's youthful expression fades. 'I'm sorry,' he runs a hand through his hair. 'The bus wouldn't come.'

'You always say that.' She reaches for him.

'I'm sorry,' he repeats, bowing to meet her lips.

'You always say that too. Consistently late.'
'Consistently apologetic.' They kiss.

The first time they ever kissed, she remembers, she was ner-
vous and clumsy. They can just about laugh at it now. An old
friend from college had dragged her along to a lunchtime
poetry reading in St George's Crypt. She had puckered, peck-
ing at his unfamiliar mouth like a chicken. All she could think
was that his lips were fatter and warmer than Harry's. She
agreed to see him again on the condition that he never put
her in a poem.

'But women are always wanting me to write them in,' he
said. 'Why not?'

'Because I would never be able to do the same for you.'

'I wouldn't mind.'

'Exactly my point,' she flirted. 'I don't want you turning
me into an object—'

'A subject,' he corrected.

'Even worse.'

'OK, I promise. Meet me for dinner next Thursday.'

'Where?'

'I'll phone.'

'I'm married, by the way.'

'So am I.'

She hesitated, watching him as they seemed to step away
from their bodies, like referees inspecting a frozen punch.
Behind her a restive queue of women in bohemian necklaces
clutched newly purchased copies of *The Frog-Lily* to its breast.
Chairs scraped in the background; mineral water fizzed, bottles of wine uncorked. The interval had only just begun.

David and Catherine circled, inspected, were satisfied.

'Ring me in the day. Late morning,' she said, writing numbers on the back of her ticket. 'Is your wife here now?'

'No. We're separated.'

'You're difficult to live with?'

'Apparently.'

'Me too.' They smiled, they kissed. The bohemian necklaces blushed.

David and Catherine make love quickly in the empty house. Afterwards he goes upstairs to shower while she runs a bath. He finishes first and sometimes comes back down to watch her wash, occasionally even getting in with her and soaping her back. Catherine swears, laughing, that if he ever writes a poem about a woman in a bath she will leave him. Sometimes he just dries and dresses and waits for her in the study. There is always a shared moment of embarrassment the first time they look at each other after sex.

Catherine runs down to the kitchen to fix them drinks. David stays where he is and gazes at the bookshelves, at his own five poetry collections, in pride of place and chronological progression, the slim spines leaning slightly against the dog-shaped bookend Sarah made in pottery the year before.

'What are you looking at?' she asks, gliding back, ice clinking in tumblers, but from the angle of his head she can tell.

'Nothing special,' he says.

They talk a bit about his writing. They wonder what to do next. Catherine has seen a flat for sale nearby and she thinks it would be perfect for him, but she isn't sure how to broach the subject. David has already spotted the estate agent's magazine lying open on her desk. He waits to see if she will dare to mention it.

Usually he has gone by the time Sarah and Harry get back. Sarah goes straight to bed and waits for her mother to come up and say good night. Sometimes there will be a row first, which Sarah listens to carefully; slammed doors do not cause her undue concern, but the catastrophe of glass shattering will bring her running down in tears.

'Mum,' she pleads from the doorway; she has brought a teddy bear too for special effect.

'Broken glass,' says Harry. 'Mind your feet.'

'I can't take much more of this,' her mother threatens. Sarah backs out.

'Go to bed, we'll be up in a mo'.'

'Are you OK?' Sarah whispers in the dark as Catherine pushes open her bedroom door, its wooden edge brushing swiftly against the carpet.

She stands like a vision in the fan of corridor light. 'Not really.' She sniffs and bends over her daughter's now-sleepy face, stroking her hair.

'What were you and Dad arguing about?'

'The usual things. It's not important.'

'Is David coming back tomorrow?' she asks. Usually talking about David cheers her up.

'No, he says he's got to work. He was sorry to miss you, though.'

'Did he read my story?'

'No. I'm sorry. There wasn't time.' She dabs her eyes with a tissue, then kisses Sarah on the cheek. 'There's never enough time.'

'Which way now?'

'Straight on, I think.' David glances back from the signpost to the map on his knee where red and blue lines wriggle across from the top right corner of the page like veins in a biology textbook. He looks at the signpost again and sighs, runs a hand through his hair. They are obviously on a completely different road to the one his index finger has been tracing, in fits and starts, for the last ten minutes. *Why do cartographers always make their city centres yellow?* he wonders, thinking of home. *The colour of hope and sunshine. Buttercups.*

Sarah leans forwards. 'Are we lost?' she asks in a cheerful voice.

'Of course not. Here, give me the map.'

It is Catherine's birthday and they have been in the car since eight o'clock, their picnic shifting from side to side in the boot with every unexpected bend in the road. Through a gap in the hedge Sarah sees a wheatfield, sloping up gently to the foot of a wood. The South Downs seem to stretch as far as the horizon. 'It's very picturesque,' she encourages, remembering David's first excuse for having taken them off the main road.

'Isn't it,' he agrees.

'Quiet everyone. I need to concentrate.' The car inches forward, swinging left as they circle in one. 'We're going back.'

'To London?'

'To the A286.' Catherine steps on the accelerator, gravel crunches.

Now sunlight streams across the opposite side of the car and Sarah shifts into the shade. She levers open the back-seat window and sticks her fingers through the crack, wiggling them in the wind. For a long time nobody says anything.

The beach, when they get to it, seems deserted. The tide is out. A sequence of groynes steps wearily down to the water's edge and the shingle rasps. Little waves roll up crooked in the sharp west wind and empty themselves at the feet of seagulls. Black clouds cast shadow over the distant headland. Shivering, Catherine stumbles back to the car park for her jacket. Sarah and David head for the nearest triangle but someone else is already there, a fat man in swimming trunks, sunbathing in the lee. He keeps his eyes tight shut as they approach, pretending to be asleep. His belly and chest are pink and forested with fine blond hairs. Sarah looks back towards the car park.

'Oh well,' says David, picking up the hamper. 'Let's try the next one.' They clatter off, slipping and twisting as the pebbles shift beneath their feet.

'Why do men have hairy chests?' she asks, when they have finally settled down behind a shelter of their own. Buttoned up like a Christmas caroller, her mother struggles along the crest of the beach towards them.

'Everyone has hair all over, it just doesn't show on some people.' David picks up a pebble and turns it slowly in the palm of his hand. He lifts it to his shoulder, testing the weight. 'Have you brought your swimming costume?'

Sarah nods. 'Mum's got it. Have you?'

'Yes, but I'm not going in.'

'Why not?'

'It's far too cold.' He straightens his arm like a shot-putter and the pebble catapults away, cracking in two as it lands. Sarah gets up to find the pieces. She runs her fingers over the smooth grey flint inside and fits them back together. The seam is barely visible.

'I know, let's play a trick on Mum.'

She watches, absorbed, as David unfolds a packet of tobacco and sprinkles the dark brown strands onto a rizla. He rolls it into a delicate-looking cigarette and strikes a match; it gutters out, immediately, in the wind. Crouching deeper into the crack between shingle and groyne, he tries again.

'What are you doing?' Catherine flops down on the stones beside him, wiping the hair from her eyes. It is already thick and greasy with salt.

'Running out of matches,' he replies from inside his jacket. A puff of smoke escapes between the denim lapels.

'A single tree can make a hundred thousand matches,' announces Sarah, 'and a single match can burn a hundred thousand trees.'

Catherine rests her head on David's lap and gazes at the sky.

After lunch the grown-ups take off their shoes and socks and wander lazily towards the sea while Sarah guards her mother's handbag. The tide has turned and now the end of the groyne is underwater. Yellow froth bobs on the waves and the sun dips in and out between the clouds. Catherine paddles, scampering back when the water threatens the folded-up ends of her trousers, shrieking with laughter to make sure David knows how much she is enjoying herself. They admire each other's naked feet, white and soft-looking against the flinty brown pebbles. The gleaming, blood-red nail varnish she painted on the night before has chipped.

Suddenly she sprays him, once, twice, asking for a fight, and he lunges after her. They pantomime chase, Catherine dodging and feinting like a matador. Catching her at last, he swings her into his arms and staggers to the water.

'Stop, you'll drop me,' she pleads, thrashing.

'No I won't.'

'Stop it, please.'

'Don't you trust me?' He wades deeper in, ignoring the waves which are splashing, now, halfway up his thighs.

'I don't trust anyone.'

'Why shouldn't I drop you then?'

She can feel his warm chest through her T-shirt, the beat of his heart. Everything has gone serious. 'To show you love me?'

'If you won't trust me, how can I?'

He seems to be loosening his grip, growing tired. Fleetingly she worries about his back. 'OK, OK, I'm sorry. I trust you!'

He stops. He hoists her higher in his arms. Although he is staring, now, right into her passionate dark eyes, all he can see is a reflection of his own face, bulging like a face in a spoon. 'Let go of my neck.'

Looping the handbag round her shoulders, Sarah hurries

down to the shore to see what's happening. The sun goes in
again and it starts to rain.

They trudge in single file back to the car and sit in it, watching as raindrops spit and trickle against the glass. Their damp
clothes steam. Sarah draws wobbly circles in the condensation
and mirror-writes 'Help, we can't get out' on the rear window for a joke.

'Where are we going now? I'm bored,' she says at last,
breaking the silence. Her mother switches the engine on.
The windscreen wipers swish and suddenly the car park, its
portaloos, its roadside café, its litter bins, fall into focus.
Aimlessly, they set off for Worthing, a journey of roundabouts
and queues.

The far side of Climping they pass a funfair, its merry-go-
round lights flashing off and on to the sound of Ultravox, a
few bedraggled holiday-makers wandering from stand to
stand. Catherine pulls over and they all climb out, Sarah running ahead in her excitement. At the beefburger van she stops
and waits. David and Catherine walk into view round the
back of a shooting gallery. They are not holding hands. They
look in opposite directions. The sun is still lost in cloud but
her mother has put on her dark glasses. Her thin, pale lips
have almost disappeared. She's fighting back tears. David fishes
in his pocket for change and picks up an air-rifle, fitting it to
his shoulder. There are four of them, chained to the counter
in a row. In front of him a mother duck and seven tin ducklings cog slowly from right to left. The proprietor stands back
and folds her arms as David aims and fires. There is a ping and
one of the ducklings flips over. Catherine looks away.

'Can I have some money, Mum?'

'What for?'

'Candyfloss.'

'No, you'll make yourself sick.'

'I won't. I'm really hungry.'

'But you've only just had lunch.'

There is another ping, and another.

'Please, please.'

Catherine stares coldly into her daughter's imploring face. 'Here,' she mutters, clicking open the purse and taking out two pound coins. 'Do what you want.'

'Thanks.' Sarah examines them with disbelief. 'Will you come on one of the rides with me?'

'No, Sarah, I already feel peculiar. Ask *him*.'

David has won a piece of blue fur glued into the shape of a sausage. The stuck-on eyes and four felt feet suggest that it is meant to resemble a member of the animal kingdom, though it's impossible to tell which. 'Happy Birthday,' he grins, handing it to Catherine. Sarah leads them towards the Dodgems.

'Sorry,' says the man in the ticket-booth. 'No unaccompanied children.'

About to run out of petrol, they pull off into a village, looking for a service station. Catherine struggles with the fuel cap and David gets out to stretch his legs. Sarah wanders into the shop. In the middle of the back wall where the newspapers and magazines are displayed a scuffed door opens out into the stockroom. She steals a glance at the shop assistant, embarrassed to ask. Joan Collins pouts provocatively from the cover of the *Radio Times* and suddenly she is aware of a whole row of magazine faces, men and women with touched-up, knowing smiles, all looking at her.

'Excuse me, may I use your toilet?'

'Through there.' He points at the door without looking up from his newspaper.

There is a calendar on the wall above the sink which Sarah stares at, fascinated, as she washes her hands. She has never seen a peep-hole bra before.

'You like that, do you?'

She turns around. David is grinning at her ruthlessly.

'No.' Blushing, she pushes past him into the shop.

One day Catherine finds a hair in the shower. It is black, 42 centimetres long and kinked into peculiar curls as if it has been badly ironed. Without a moment's hesitation she phones Harry at work. 'What hair colour is your current whore?'

'Catherine, is that you?'

'Well?'

'I'm in a meeting. I wouldn't have time to talk to you about the end of the world, let alone the colour of my girl-friend's hair.'

'Just tell me, you withholding son-of-a-bitch. It's impor-tant.'

'Blonde, like yours.' He hangs up.

Catherine pulls the hair between the tips of her fingers thoughtfully; she phones David at home. The line is engaged. She Sellotapes the hair to a piece of typing paper, which she folds in thirds and slots into an envelope. She hides it at the bottom of her underwear drawer. She tries his number again and this time someone picks up. It is a woman's voice. Catherine stiffens. 'Can I speak to David?'

'Hold on. I'll just get him for you. Who shall I say it is?'

Catherine hears herself say her name and surname and a long pause follows, then David's voice comes on at the other end. He sounds surprised to hear from her. 'Who was that?' she asks, trying to be rational.

'The cleaner.'

'The cleaner? How can you afford a cleaner?'

'Didn't I mention? I sold the last few acres of my inheritance last week, and splashed out on, among other things, a cleaner. I thought you'd approve. You're always complaining about this place. Honestly, next time you come round you won't be able to recognise it. The walls have actually changed colour.' He sounds unusually cheerful. Catherine burns.

'Can I ask you something?' she says, recklessly.

'Of course.'

'Do you love me?'

'What do you think?'

'I think I think you do.'

'Well then, I must.'

'And you're not having an affair?'

'I'm having an affair with you. One is enough.' He hesitates. The lightness has evaporated from their voices. 'Why do you ask?'

'Nothing.'

'What do you mean "nothing"?'

'I mean it's nothing. Forget it. I'm premenstrual. I needed reassurance, you know . . .' she tails off hopefully. He does not offer to come round. They agree to meet on Saturday as usual and hang up. Catherine removes the envelope from its hiding place and throws it away.

*

Sarah lets herself in after school to find the house apparently empty. She wanders from floor to floor, calling, 'Mum, where are you, Mum?' but no one answers. She must have gone out, she decides, not bothering to look for a note. In her room she changes out of her school uniform and unpacks her satchel, scattering lunch-box, books and felt-tip pens across the carpet. She goes downstairs to watch TV and sits through a not particularly exciting episode of *Blue Peter* in which the winners of their 'design a stained-glass window' competition are announced. She makes herself toast and jam. Outside it is raining. Through the gap in the hedge she can see Joshua, a golden retriever, standing alone in the middle of the communal garden. His owners have forgotten to let him in. Suddenly the floor creaks overhead. Shivers rush up Sarah's spine as she imagines ghosts.

In her mother's room, Sarah's eyes grow slowly accustomed to the dark. In the crack between the pale blue duvet and matching pillow she is relieved to see her crumpled face. 'Mum,' she whispers, 'are you asleep?' Since Catherine does not reply, Sarah tiptoes closer to the bed. She listens for breathing and, fearful that her heart may have for some unknown reason stopped, touches her cheek.

Catherine's body seizes up as if she has been stung. 'What do you want?' she asks in her ordinary, wide-awake voice.

Sarah shrugs. 'Why are you in bed?'

'I had some bad news.'

'What?'

'Mind your own business.'

Sarah steps back, hurt; normally her mother tells her everything. 'What's for supper?'

'I don't know. Your father won't be in 'til late – we could just have cereal if you like.'

'OK.'

'Leave me alone now, will you? And if the phone rings, don't answer it.'

'What if it's David?'

'It won't be.'

Five hours later the floor creaks again. Sarah jumps up to turn the television off; it's past her bedtime and she doesn't want to be yelled at. Catherine bursts into the room. 'Get your shoes on, we're going out.' She has thrown a long beige mackintosh over her nightie and slipped her bare feet into a pair of red high heels. Foundation and blusher have been reapplied to her swollen, tear-scalded face. A fat black leather bag hangs from her shoulder and her left hand clutches a ring of keys. 'Quickly!'

'Where are we going?'

'Never you mind. Just hurry up and do as you're told.'

They stand on the pavement, Catherine fiddling with the car lock. Sarah doesn't remember ever having been out this late on a weekday before. The rain has stopped, the street smells faintly of damp garbage and the sky is brown. Two young men walk past. Sarah watches them eyeing her mother's shoes and cringes with embarrassment.

'Get in the back and put your seat belt on.' They accelerate noisily towards the main road, heading north. Through the rear-view mirror Sarah can see the anger in her mother's face begin to loosen as she races towards the park. Driving always makes her feel better, more in control of things. 'Sit back, will you. I can't see a thing.'

'Are we going to Dad's office?' she asks, as they swing onto the Marylebone Road and slow into a queue of brake-lights.

'No.' Dimly lit office blocks and red-brick mansion flats glide by. In silence they pass the Planetarium, Madame Tussauds, the Royal Academy of Music. Sarah catches the eye of a taxi-driver they pull alongside just before the under-pass, and the two cars leap-frog all the way to King's Cross. The taxi-driver winks at her and chuckles every time they pass; his three chins wobble in the street light; his passengers wear trilbys and look bewildered.

They overtake an empty bus and turn left down a long, dark avenue which Sarah doesn't recognise. The pavements are plastered with soggy newspapers; beer-cans block the gut-ters. They follow signs to Hampstead, weave between graffiti-covered railway bridges, cross the canal. The streets seem narrower and darker. Sarah has no idea where they are. The houses are smaller. Suddenly they stop. The car reverses sharply into the pavement. The engine cuts.

'Where are we, Mum?' The headlights flick off, abandon-ing them.

'This is where David lives,' says Catherine. Sarah follows her across the road and in through a garden gate. They feel their way down four steep, concrete steps by the side of the house. It's a basement flat.

Catherine rings the bell, stepping back to wait. When nobody answers she rings again, twice.

'Maybe he's not there. Let's go home.'

'Of course he's there.' Her mother rings the bell again. 'I know you're there, so open the door, you bastard,' she yells, kicking it. She stops for a second to readjust her hair, then kicks it again.

When David finally opens the door, holding the frame with one hand so that it won't swing too wide and let the cold in, his chest is naked.

'Hello,' he says, looking at Sarah. 'How are you?'

'We wanted to see your nice clean flat,' says Catherine. 'Can we come in?'

David looks uncomfortable. 'No,' he says at last, staring at his toes, 'you can't. There's someone here.'

The journey home breaks Sarah's heart. She sits in the front this time, and pretends to be watching the road. Tears roll silently down Catherine's face, which shines as stripes of neon flicker across the car. She is driving slowly now, lingering at traffic lights, hesitating at junctions like a learner, unsure of whether or not it's safe to go. She has lost her anger; she doesn't seem to be able to remember how to get home. Eventually they pull over and look at the map. They have been driving round in circles. An Italian-looking woman with long black hair crosses the road in front of them. Catherine opens her door, leans out over the pavement and vomits. Sarah can't think of anything to say except, 'Mum, don't cry. Please.'

It is nearly eleven o'clock when they get back and Harry is furious with waiting. Catherine walks straight up to her room. 'Where the hell have you been?' he calls after her. Sarah puts herself to bed.

The following morning David appears on the doorstep just as Catherine is about to take her to school. 'We'll have to wait

for him to go,' she says starkly, ushering her daughter back
into the living room. She knows it's him from the denim
jacket, she will not look at his liar's face.

'But I'll be late.'

'So what?'

'I'll be sent to Mrs Oakley!'

'I'm not leaving this house until he's gone and I'm not
having you walk to school on your own and that's final.' They
sit in the conservatory.

Sarah looks at her watch. 'Mum, can I go to the loo?' she
says. Catherine nods. Sarah closes the door behind her and lets
David in.

'Hello,' he grins foolishly.

'Hi,' says Sarah with disapproval. 'Mum won't take me to
school unless you go away—' but David is not listening. He
pushes past her into the conservatory, where Catherine stares
at him with disbelief. She rises slowly to her feet and picks up
her empty coffee cup. Even as it whistles through the air she
wonders what, exactly, he will need to promise before she
takes him back.

Trailing across the brittle playground, past huddles of hungry juniors dealing football stickers, and girlie gangs already dressed for Brownies, Sarah stares into a blur of parents and children waiting on the far side of the fence and suddenly realises, with a start of guilt, that she has looked straight through her mother. She looks again to make sure: Catherine has never been so tanned, she is wearing a new coat and stands apart from the rest, close to the fence with her hands in her pockets and a dark purple scarf wrapped twice around her neck. Her daughter has been sent to the local state primary as a matter of principle. That Catherine would never make friends with any of the other parents is Sarah's one, long-standing grievance. She runs to her, but even after the hugs and kisses still feels oddly disconcerted.

They walk home briskly through the wan February sunshine, automatically reaching out to hold hands on the zebra crossing, as though some gesture of mutual tenderness is required. Sarah stares at her mother's black leather boots as they step in and out of sight above the cracks in the pavement. Catherine fixes her eyes on the post box at the end of the road and begins to explain why she hasn't brought her a present.

Swallowing the disappointment, Sarah takes her mother's hand again and holds it tight the rest of the way home. 'You're very brown,' she says, jumping up and down on the doorstep to keep warm as Catherine fiddles with her keys.

It had taken David no more than five days to persuade her to try to forgive him. Finally accepting his sincere apologies, his promise never to be unfaithful again, with hints of a proposal of marriage thrown in for good measure, they came to terms. The treaty was sealed with a two-week holiday in Jamaica, a last-minute honeymoon cancellation, and they returned to England reconciled.

David stays away that night, and for supper Catherine makes seafood pasta, Sarah's favourite dish. Sarah clears the table and carries up plates, cutlery, glasses and candles. She puts on her favourite piece of music, Vivaldi's *Four Seasons*, which she remembers listening to on the radio one summer with the conservatory windows open onto the garden and a terrifying, real-life thunder storm distorting the reception. Catherine calls her down to the kitchen to help drain the rigatoni.

She wants to know more about what Sarah has been up to during her absence. Did her father feed her properly? Did she finish her history project? What did they do at the weekend? But, describing Harry's successful Boat Show impersonation of a millionaire in search of his ideal yacht, Sarah realises that her mother is not really listening.

'Mum,' she breaks off. 'Are you OK? Aren't you hungry?'

Catherine looks at her plate and wonders, for the hundredth time, if David has really gone home as, climbing into separate taxis at Victoria, he said he would. She doesn't believe him any more, not a word he says. It feels as though they have never been away together and she can't remember any of his promises.

'Not really,' she replies, examining the pink question mark of a prawn with her fork. 'I'm not used to eating at this time.'

'Shall I make you a hot water bottle? Are you cold?'

'No, Sarah, stay where you are and eat your supper. I'm fine.' She stands up and carries her plate to the bin, to scrape away the leftovers. 'Do you mind if I turn this off?' she glances at the tape recorder.

'Not if you don't,' answers Sarah with her mouth full.

'It's giving me a headache.'

'Shall I get you an aspirin?'

'No! Stay where you are, and stop mothering me for God's sake! I can get it.' She rushes out of the room in tears.

Sarah listens to the footsteps trudge upstairs, across the creaky bedroom floor and into the bathroom; she covers the pasta bowl with clingfilm and puts it in the fridge.

Catherine comes up to say good night. She sits on the edge of Sarah's bed, smoothing the covers. The room smells minty, of toothpaste, and the rumble of traffic on Fulham Road seeps in with cold air through the window crack.

'Daddy phoned. He's going to sleep over at the office tonight. He asked me to kiss you good night from him.'

Sarah smiles.

'I'm sorry things have been difficult,' Catherine begins. 'David and I talked a lot on holiday – we've decided to try again, we want to spend more time together.'

'Oh good,' says Sarah, drowsily.

'Tomorrow I'm going to sort out a cupboard for him, you can help me if you like, so he has somewhere to keep his clothes and books when he comes round. We decided he should sleep here sometimes.'

Sarah nods.

'But I don't want you to think this means I'll have any less time for you – we can do things all three of us together.'

'OK.'

'You've got to understand,' Catherine very gently wipes the sleep from her daughter's eye with the corner of her sleeve, 'that I love David in a completely different way to the way I love you. When you're grown up maybe you'll know what I mean. Loving him doesn't make me love you any less.'

'I missed you.'

'I know, I missed you too. Things should be better from now on.'

Harry and Catherine push their chairs back from the table and stand up. 'I'll get it,' says Catherine. The doorbell has gone and David is expected. Harry sits down again and smiles quizzically at his daughter. He removes his glasses, polishes them on an undone navy blue cuff and slips them back into position. They have had a difficult morning and he considers David's arrival untimely at best. Waiting in the hall are the two suitcases and four cardboard boxes Sarah has watched him pack. There are tears hiding in the corners of his eyes. He looks around the sun-filled kitchen. A string of teenagers on their way to the cinema at the end of the road walks past the front window, chatting and swinging their rucksacks. Next door's white camellia brushes against the glass at the back. Through the gap in the fence he can see into the garden square, where Joshua stands in the middle of a group of children, watching their ball with infinite patience. He wonders sadly whether he will get to see the wisteria in bloom this year; the tears are playing grandmother's footsteps, he shakes himself.

'Don't mope. It's not forever,' he says to Sarah cheerily. 'Otherwise I'd be taking a whole lot more!'

The door clicks open and David sidles in, followed by Catherine. The two men shake hands, muttering heartily. 'Off on holiday?' asks David, nodding towards the bags in the hall. 'The plane will never take off with that little lot!'

Harry glances at Catherine, surprised. 'No, I'm just moving some stuff over to the office for a while. Moving out sort of thing – I rather assumed you knew.'

Catherine butts in. 'We only decided last night . . .'

Now it's David's turn to look surprised. 'I'm lost for words.'

'And you a poet!' Harry laughs weakly. 'Well, I should be going. Sarah, want to come and help me settle in?'

Sarah runs to fetch her shoes and David slumps into her empty chair.

'Do you like ice-cream?'

Sarah stared happily through the window as Marion manoeuvred into a space. It was market day and they were lucky to have found one so near the shops. An old woman with a brown tartan trolley clattered in front of the car and waited, one hand resting on the bonnet, for the traffic to stop.

'The post office sells fantastic ice-creams. If we're quick.' They opened their doors. Sarah carried the plastic bags, crushed into a squeezy crackling ball. When Marion reached out for her at the kerb, she pretended to be looking at the houses on the far side of the square. She didn't want to hold hands; she was perfectly old enough to take care of herself. Her father had given her a five-pound note.

It was bright. Sunlight mirrored the passers-by in shop windows: women with prams, children with dogs, men with shopping lists, middle-aged tourists in long shorts searching for antiques. Pensioners crossed over to walk in the shade. The woman with the trolley trundled into a bakery. Later they found themselves three behind her in the butcher's queue.

'Are you sure you'll eat liver, pet?' Marion was saying. 'A

lot of children won't.' Sarah unscrunched a second bag. From a hidden alcove at the back of the shop came the deliberate thud, thud of cleaver on chopping board. The butcher returned with a small package under his arm. He threw it onto the scales and wiped his hands.

'Excuse me. How much are these?' They had gone in looking for wellington boots but the penknives caught Sarah's eye immediately. Ryders was the most expensive shop in the town, it occupied all four floors of a red-brick Georgian building next to the grocer's and was carpeted throughout in a dark mustardy brown into which, it was hoped, the mud-prints of its distinguished farming clientele would blend seamlessly. Marion was weaving a path between the Barbour carousels and didn't look back. The assistant began his off-by-heart Swiss Army mantra. Sarah listened with absolute concentration.

'Have you got any for five pounds?' she asked, when he had finished.

'These,' he dipped below the polished glass counter and pulled out a drawer, 'but they only have the one application.'

She opened the stiff blade. It was already going rusty at the hinge. 'I'll think about it.' She turned away.

Marion rushed across the shop floor. Her face was red and her earrings twitched like string-puppets. 'Where were you?' she whispered furiously, marching Sarah by her elbow into the next room. 'I've been going out of my mind!'

'I was—'

'I've been looking for you everywhere. Where were you?'

'I was looking at—'

She shook her. 'Thank God you're all right. Don't ever do that again – you promise?'

'Do what?'

'What if I hadn't found you?'

'I'd have waited by the car.'

Marion drew breath. She glanced round the room and absentmindedly slipped one hand into a sheepskin mitten. She mustn't make a scene. After all, children were always getting themselves lost in department stores; that's what the Tannoys are for, she told herself. 'OK.' She took the mitten off again, returning it to the display precisely. There was a long pause. 'Maybe I overreacted. Let's try again, shall we? And this time—'

'Sorry,' Sarah followed her back through the shop, past the penknives. 'Look!'

'What now?'

As if in a trance, Sarah approached the cabinet. 'Aren't they cool!'

'I had one of those once.'

'Did you?' Her eyes lit up. 'Which?'

Marion inspected the case. Unopened they all looked the same, like a collection of long, red chloroformed insects. She shook her head.

'Oh please! I'll pay you back – this one's only twelve ninety-five.' The assistant had returned. He fished out the key from his pocket and unlocked the cabinet. 'Please!'

'I'm already buying you a pair of boots.'

'Yes but this wouldn't be like a present. I'll give you five pounds now and the rest next time Dad comes up.'

The assistant buried his smile and Marion sighed. She

tucked her hair behind her ears, jolting the silver beads. 'What do you want it for, anyway?'

Sarah shrugged. 'It's useful. Oh please.'

Sarah chose chocolate chip, while Marion, still recovering from the shock of nearly having lost her, agonised between lemon sorbet (less fattening) and strawberry. In the end she went with Sarah's choice, telling herself that children know about these things. They leaned against the side of the car in the sunshine and watched the market traders clear up, their own shopping safely stowed in the boot. A small Ryders bag lay casually on the passenger seat.

The sun was going down as they arrived back home. Blackbirds hopped from molehill to molehill and ignored the car. Ollie barked frantically, then leapt up at Sarah, plastering her with kisses when they finally got through the door.

Someone had phoned. Marion regarded the flashing red light suspiciously. Jamie had insisted on them getting an answer-machine, for work, he said. She revelled in their isolation and would rather not have known. She pressed rewind and listened as Harry's voice, tired and exasperated, crackled from the low-tech speaker. 'Hello, Marion, Jamie. Just wanted to have a word with one of you – I'll try again later. Love to Sarah.' Marion sighed, rewound the message a second time and erased it.

It was chillier indoors than out, and gloomy shadows skulked in the corners, refusing to budge even after the lights had been turned on. Sarah came in, hovered tentatively, wondering whether she ought to lend a hand, then ran off into the garden to examine her penknife in greater detail.

Ollie followed. Lumped together unbeautifully on the kitchen table, the bulging carrier bags demanded attention. Marion looked at her watch. She didn't want to unpack the shopping; suddenly she would rather have let it rot than bend over to open the fridge. She sat, with her back to the windows, and stared at Jamie's grandmother's tallboy and the whitewashed walls on either side and tried not to cry. The oven clock ticked, the ancient fridge stammered into a hum.

She wandered upstairs to run a bath. Jamie wouldn't be back for at least an hour. The hot tap squeaked and a dribble of scalding water slipped down the side of the tub. Pipes gurgled and, as the dribble grew into a steady jet, the bathroom clouded with steam. Bath salts foamed in the current and the water turned a deep greeny blue. She sat on the edge of the bath and concentrated on not thinking about Toby, but the homesickness – that was the only way she knew how to describe it – followed her everywhere. The bath would take ten minutes to run, at least. If only Jamie would come home. Flicking on the cheerful yellow light for company, she drifted into their room, slipped off her trainers and crawled, fully dressed, between the sheets.

Harry snapped his address book shut and listened to the number ring, pencilling empty circles on the back of an inter-office memorandum. Again he pictured the hospital, the doctor's brisk white coat receding, vanishing back along the same interminable corridor from which, five minutes before, he had appeared, a tiny dot in the perspective, swing doors fluttering silently. His father used to walk like that, and check his watch with the same exaggerated gesture. Maybe this was why he hated hospitals, doctors, the NHS.

Nothing to do with Catherine had ever been simple, he had thought. He might have known she'd run away. He had sniffed the flowers, freesias this time, then leaned them carefully, up for grabs, against the battered wall and hurried home, where his key turned easily in the lock and the front door sprang open. A copy of the *Guardian* lay on the mat. At least she hadn't bolted him out, he had told himself, climbing the stairs.

He had called her name quietly and knocked on the bedroom door but there was no answer. He pushed it open and peered into the darkness, calling her name again, less quietly. He looked in the bathroom and the study. His old room upstairs, Sarah's room and the shower room were empty too. She's just popped out for a pint of milk, he told himself. He sat on the stairs for a moment and tried not to panic.

Back in the bedroom he drew back the curtains, searching for clues. Grey morning light settled on the bed. There were long, thin crisscrosses of dried blood smeared across the duvet cover and sheet. Perhaps she had left a letter. The bed was cold, the wad of tissues shoved under the pillow dry. On the bedside table there were razor blades, an alarm clock, a felt-tip pen and a bottle of aspirin; he rattled it – almost full. No note, no sign of her handbag. He crouched on his knees to look under the bed. The black leather suitcase he had bought her one Harrods sale was gone. In the bathroom he noticed her make-up bag missing too and, for a second, allowed himself to smile. He flushed two handfuls of tissues down the loo and stripped the bed, folding the sheets neatly and depositing them in the washing room.

A pair of curling tongs was balanced on top of the phone directory on her desk in the study. Below them, a sheet of paper purporting to be the last will and testament of Catherine Ellis read: 'Everything to my daughter Sarah, excepting only my 3-tape set of *Don Giovanni*, which is to be given to David Finch in memory of our time together.' Instinctively, Harry looked for a signature and a date, but there was neither. He wanted to scrunch it into a hard, tight, spiky ball and ram it down her throat. Instead he had phoned the newsagent's and cancelled the paper. He had double-locked the front door after him and driven to work. What else was there for one to do, in a situation like this?

He doodled faster, he resented having to make the call. The

man had humiliated him enough already. Somewhere, in a
basement flat he couldn't even begin to imagine, in Kentish
Farm, North London, the telephone rang and rang. Harry's
circles grew tighter and darker, jerking out from the bottom
right corner of the page. They began to shine. The ringing
stopped and a woman cleared her throat.

'Hello?' She sounded guarded, surprised.

'I'd like to speak to David Finch. Is this the wrong number?'

'No.' The receiver banged. 'It's a man,' she shouted across
the room. Footsteps approached the telephone.

'Hello?'

'It's Harry – Ellis.' He paused. 'I wondered if Catherine had
called you recently, or—'

'No.'

'Or if you'd seen her?'

'No,' David sighed. 'What's happened? Is she lost?'

'Oh, she'll turn up.' Harry tried to sound confident. 'I
wonder, though, if she does get in touch, could you let me
know?'

'All right. Do I have your number?'

'You've probably thrown it away.'

'Steady on—'

'Sorry.'

David seemed to be shuffling pieces of paper. 'Yes, here it
is. All right.' He waited carefully. 'Anything else?'

'No.'

'Well, goodbye then.'

'Bye.' Harry replaced the receiver and stopped doodling.
He reached across his desk to pull the blind. His reflection was

beginning to annoy him. Good old Harry. So hard-working. So cheerful. He pushed back his chair and went to the drinks cabinet. Aside from the mattress and a coat-stand it was the only piece of furniture he had taken. Three plates, three knives and forks and seven glasses, all used, jostled for space on top. He reached inside and poured himself a gin and tonic.

'Sarah, love, Dad phoned last night.' Jamie had finished breakfast and stood, ready for work, with his back to the sink. Sarah was disappointed. 'You were fast asleep, pet. He said not to wake you. He sends his love.'

'How's Mum?'

'The doctors say she's out of hospital.' He cleared his throat.

'Good.' She munched hurriedly and swallowed. 'Can I ring her?'

'The thing is, pet,' Marion took over. They should have expected this. 'She's not at home, so you'll have to wait for her to ring you.'

'Didn't she leave a number?'

'No.'

'Where's she gone?'

'We don't know, exactly.'

'But when's she coming back?'

'Sarah, love, she'll come back when she's feeling better,' said Jamie gently. 'She probably just needs to spend a bit of time on her own.'

Sarah stared into her bowl of Weetabix. It slipped out of

focus, doubling. She couldn't bear to think of her mother like that, all alone. 'Can I phone Dad?'

'Not now, love, he'll be working.'

'He won't mind.'

'Best not to disturb him, pet. Let's try tonight. Maybe he'll have heard from Mummy by then.' Jamie looked at his watch. He was going to be late. 'Anyway, there's something I want to show you.'

'Now?'

He nodded, encouraging her flicker of interest.

'What?'

'It's a secret. Come with me.'

They wiggled into their boots and followed Ollie out into the yard. It was cloudy and still outside, and the fields seemed very flat and green. They brushed through the heavy grass towards the stream, but instead of crossing the footbridge Jamie turned left and, putting a finger to his lips, tiptoed with exaggerated caution along the bank.

'We're in luck,' he whispered back to her. 'The water's clear.'

He beckoned and crouched on his heels. Sarah did the same. Below them the stream widened out into a small pool, which gurgled happily. A cluster of bubbles floated in the current, winking.

'Look down there, a little to the right of your feet,' he pointed. 'Slowly, though – if you lean over too far you'll scare it away.'

Through the bright reflections of branches and clouds, Sarah could just make out the bottom of the stream, about two feet down, pale and sandy, and marbled with seams of black sediment. Suddenly, exactly where Jamie had said to look, she saw a fish, swimming on the spot, nose first, massaging itself in the current, twisting from side to side like a short thick snake. It was brown and freckled with a pale belly, about one and a half hand-spans long. She could even see its speckled fins, fanned out for balance. Jamie looked over her shoulder.

'See how sensitive it is,' he whispered. 'Lean over some more, ve-ry slow-ly.'

Almost at once the trout took fright. Its belly flashed, kicking up small whirls of sand and, when the water cleared again, the pool was empty. Sarah looked upset.

'Will it come back?' she worried.

'Of course,' said Jamie standing up and stretching his sore knees. 'This is its home. I've got to go to work now. See you later.' He tramped back up the lawn, turning once to see Sarah poised, her bright face hidden behind a curtain of thick yellow hair, exactly as he had left her.

'Do you live here?' The boy seemed to have materialised out of thin air. Sarah jolted to her feet, blanching, and let go of her stone. Murky water splashed her already mud-streaked shins. He laughed, jumping back from the edge of the pool.

'No,' she said defensively. 'I'm not a frog, you know.'

'In the house, stupid.' He had a thin freckled face and sunburnt lips, he could only smile a bit at a time. His pale brown hair was very short – almost shaved.

'Oh. No. Sort of. It's my mother's cousin's house.'

The boy seemed to be impressed by this genealogy and waited, staring up at the yard, for her to explain. Sarah looked over her shoulder to see if Marion was about. 'I'm only staying for a while. I live in London. What's your name?'

'George. What's yours?'

'Sarah.'

'Your feet must be freezing.'

The face of the pool was calm again now, small ripples wrinkled around her ankles. 'Not really. I'm building a dam. I thought you were a ghost.'

'Why?'

She shrugged. Children were supposed to go to heaven, weren't they? Toby would have liked it here. 'Do you want to help?' A half-submerged stone wall stretched ineffectually across the pool's lower mouth.

'Can't. I'm meant to be getting peas for tea.'

'From the field?'

He nodded.

'Is that allowed?'

'I should think so, it's ours!'

Sarah looked up at the ridge. Lilacy green plants stretched all the way across from the path to the wood. She hesitated, speechless for a moment at the thought of so much food. 'Can I have some?' she heard herself ask.

'OK.' He reconsidered, 'But not too many.' She waded towards him, stepped up onto the muddy bank and rolled her trouser legs down.

Together they crossed the meadow, Sarah picking her way barefoot between the thistles and nettles. A basket came into sight at the far end, hooked over a fence-post by the gate.

George climbed onto the lowest rung and heaved himself over the top, swinging his legs after and landing on the far side with a confident thud. Sarah followed awkwardly. 'How d'you do that?'

'Easy,' he answered, approaching the straggled edge of the crop, basket in hand. Tangled rows of peas stretched into the distance like a choppy lake. He stooped to the nearest plant and yanked at a pod. Sarah did the same, pulling so hard that the whole bush threatened to up-root.

'They won't come off!'

Sarah reached into her pocket and opened her hand. George's eyes lit up. 'It's got two knives, a file, a saw, a pick and scissors,' she said, unfolding the longest blade and dragging it firmly across the top of a pod. The severed plant sprang back, trembling, then fell still.

'Let's have a go.'

Sarah ran her thumb along the hinge, stripping its tiny blue peas into the palm of her hand. 'All right.' She batted a fly and stepped carefully over the crop. The soil felt like lumpy, soft sand between her toes. Not bothering to break the stem, she opened another pod and picked out its peas. Her T-shirt rippled in a sudden breath of wind and the bushes creaked. The sun came out. A cabbage-white fluttered helplessly towards the meadow.

'Come on!' George was already far ahead of her, half-lurching, half-leaping from furrow to furrow. 'I'll race you.'

In the middle of the field they stopped, dizzy, out of breath, knee-deep in an ocean of vegetables. Midges clustered above their heads. George set to work filling the basket. Sarah sat on the ground, leaned back and stared at the sky. Pink and yellow clouds banked slowly over the ridge.

The house seems strange with her father gone, not just quiet and empty but sad as well, as if he had been the only one to care for it. Blown lightbulbs go unfixed for weeks, the stair carpet grows more and more crooked, snails and dandelions steadily colonise the garden. It's funny, but Sarah notices the difference most just after she comes home from school, when he wouldn't normally have been there anyway. Without the moment of his return from work to look forward to, the remainder of the afternoon seems to drag by. She usually manages to finish her homework quickly but, since Catherine has stopped cooking and suppers come from the freezer, there is nothing much to help with in the kitchen.

She grows tired of the television for company and wishes that David would come round. In fact, if anything, they see less of him than ever. The day after Harry moves out David brings round a carrier bag of socks and shirts, and the following week he stays over for four nights running, even taking Sarah to school on the Wednesday. But the visits tail off after that. Catherine can't help wondering whether her daughter has said something to upset him, but doesn't dare ask either of them outright for fear of drawing attention to a problem that doesn't exist. David's blunt response to her carefully considered suggestion that he might like to spend more time with them in the light of his recent promises has been bad enough. She washes and irons his shirts and puts them back in the drawer.

Soon a month has gone by without him staying over once. He's continuing the affair, of course, but the thought of it doesn't seem to hurt so much the second time round. She's on the defensive now; she'd rather share him than lose him altogether, and he knows it. Her spirits sheer from compromise to desperation. She has stopped vomiting, but confines herself to her room instead, waiting for his calls, which are frequent and prolonged. They talk about work. His sixth collection's proofs have come back full of mistakes, he is seriously thinking of changing publisher. Catherine's research is going badly. They talk about their respective homes. 'Everything seems to be falling apart,' says David one night, naively. 'Even my bed's broken.'

'Really?' Catherine tries not to sound suspicious but it comes out wrong. David hesitates.

'One of the screw-on feet beneath the mattress broke. I've had to prop the corner up on telephone directories.'

'I always said you should get yourself a proper bed.'

'I think I'll have to now.'

A silent scream crescendoes at the back of Catherine's throat as she fights to control her voice. 'I've got to go now – someone at the door. Speak to you later.' She puts down the receiver and takes a deep, deep breath.

Sarah gets home from school to find the burglar alarm switched on and the second post waiting in a heap on the doormat. She goes down to the kitchen to make toast and boil the kettle. Five days' washing-up sits in the machine and left-over baked beans are hardening in a pan on the cooker. The bin is crammed with fish and chip papers from the night before, which explains why everywhere smells of vinegar and grease. There is no milk in the fridge. The house is eerily quiet. The toaster makes her jump.

It is pitch dark in her mother's room as she tentatively pushes open the door, straining her eyes to make sense of the shape in the bed. 'Mum, I've brought you a sandwich.' The duvet stirs. 'Turn the light on, will you?'

'No. And I don't want a sandwich.'

Sarah holds out the plate. 'It's cheese and tomato . . .'

'Leave it on the chest, then.'

'Do you want a hot water bottle?'

Her mother seems to consider the question. 'OK. And some water to drink.' As she fumbles on the bedside table for her glass the alarm clock falls over. 'Fuck.' She switches the light on and collapses back against the pillows as if the effort has been too much. 'Make sure you run the tap first.'

The bedside table is crowded with medicines. Sarah extracts the glass and disappears into the bathroom to refill it, returning to pass her mother her pills, bottle by bottle. This has become a ritual, but today there is a new, yellowy brown plastic container. It has a childproof lid like all the others and a label with her mother's name and the dosage instructions neatly typed on the front.

'They're anti-depressants.' Catherine has been watching her daughter's face. 'Turn the light off again, will you, it's hurting my eyes.'

'What do they do?'

'They're meant to cheer me up,' she snorts.

'I can cheer you up.'

'No you can't.'

'Yes I can. Come outside, it's a lovely day.'

'What's the point?'

Neither of them speaks for awhile, then Catherine rolls over onto her side. 'Run along, then. I'm sure you've got homework to do.'

Sometimes she phones anonymously, but David always knows it's her. He lets her listen in silence to buses and taxis thundering by outside his window, to the hum of the fridge, bluebottles looping into earshot. Quieter than these, she imagines she can hear the rush of nylon, naked feet tiptoeing towards the receiver. Soft, caressing hands. Sarah sits frozen at the far end of the room not watching the muted television. Every time she moves her mother glares at her furiously. They must be so in love, Sarah tells herself, that merely listening to each other breathe is a pleasure.

'Go and brush your hair, Sarah, you look like a jumble sale.'

It is almost like old times again: David has invited himself round for dinner. In the morning Catherine takes the car to Sainsbury's while Sarah scrubs the kitchen, and in the afternoon they cook: smoked salmon pâté for a starter, Yorkshire pudding batter, chocolate mousse. Sarah tops and tails the beans while her mother peels the potatoes and par-boils them ready for roasting. Together they plump the cushions in the drawing room and hoover the stairs. Finally, an hour and a half before he is due to arrive, they take the meat from the fridge and stuff it with slivers of chopped garlic.

Slowly the entire house fills with the smell of roast beef. Upstairs, Catherine looks at herself in the mirror. Not bad for thirty-nine, she thinks, sucking her cheeks in and stroking on shadow. The dark red powder-silk tunic she has changed into is exactly the same colour as her lipstick. She has had to Optrex her bloodshot kohl-rimmed eyes. A glass of claret stands by the hot-water tap. She knows he is probably coming to say goodbye. She has convinced herself that she can talk him out of it. She calls for her daughter. 'Go and brush your hair, Sarah, you look like a jumble sale.'

Sarah runs up to her room, puts on different clothes, and leaps back down again, swinging round the bannisters. She watches *Doctor Who* while they wait. *Doctor Who* blends into a documentary about unemployment, and after that the news comes on. In the kitchen something is burning. Catherine is still looking in the mirror, watching herself grow old. He is two and a half hours late. The bottle of wine is empty. She staggers downstairs to turn the oven off. The telephone rings.

'Don't answer it!'

Sarah's right hand trembles above the receiver. She's hungry.

'If you do I'll never speak to you again; I'll disown you; you can go and live with your father!'

Little by little the hand drops back to her side. The phone keeps ringing.

'I don't want to talk to him!'

Sarah looks wistfully at the table, laid for dinner: there are new white candles in the candlesticks, a stiff, starchy cloth, napkins, wine glasses and water glasses. They have made it look so nice. 'It might be for me . . .'

'Of course it isn't: who'd ring you at this time?'

'Dad.'

' "Dad" ,' mimics Catherine in her most sarcastic voice. 'Of course it's not your father. Why on earth would he be ringing?'

'He might want to talk to you.'

'Come off it, Sarah. It's David, phoning up to say he never wants to see me again.'

'No, it might not be.'

'Of course it is.'

Sarah rushes to the sofa where her mother is sitting, half collapsed over her drawn-together knees, her head in her hands. 'Of course he wants to see you again.' She pushes a pile of newspapers onto the floor and sits down nervously.

'Don't touch me!'

'But, Mum . . .' She can feel the tears welling up irresistibly. She blinks.

'Oh God! I can't take much more of this. Sarah, go to bed.' Suddenly Catherine is on her feet and marching over to the ringing telephone and lifting the receiver. 'I fucking hate you, you cunt,' she screams and slams it back down. Then, turning on Sarah, 'For the last time: go to BED.'

Sunshine pours through the yellow curtains, filling the room with honey light. A lone bus growls down Fulham Road and sparrows chirp in the garden. The house is quiet. London and its noises seem far away. Sarah opens her eyes and stretches her toes luxuriously. She is exactly the right temperature and has had a perfect night's sleep. Looking at her watch, she is surprised to see how early it is. The floorboards creak as she gets out of bed, crossing to the window to draw the curtains. The sky is cobalt, white clouds hover above the roofs of the houses opposite. By lunchtime it will probably be grey. She has a shower, steals downstairs, past her mother's door, and turns off the burglar alarm. Glasses, napkins and cutlery still wait hopefully on the cloth-covered table. The living room still smells of overdone meat. She looks in the fridge and wonders whether to have chocolate mousse for breakfast.

Catherine, woken by the plumbing, gets up too and staggers through to the study, bleary with Valium. She opens the window and climbs out onto the balcony, blinking down into the overgrown garden. Next door's wisteria has twisted over the wall and through the trellises; its weeping, lilac clusters droop above the gone-to-seed flower beds like a reproach. A tabby cat stares up at her malevolently, then streaks through a large hole in the fence.

The door below opens and Sarah wanders out into the sun. A large snail crunches under her shoe. Catherine watches her pick up what remains and lob it over the wall. The crushed shell lands with a crack on their neighbour's path and Sarah follows the cat through the fence, out into the garden square. She pets Joshua affectionately and searches the hedges for an appropriate stick, ducking in and out of sight as she works her way down the lawn, her T-shirt and jeans just visible through the intervening shrubs.

Catherine leans over the railing to watch but now she is so far away as to be unrecognisable, a distant, colourful blur. The sun goes in behind a cloud and she looks away. She shivers, gripping the rail with both hands, sick and dizzy at the thought of what she might do. Houses, trees and gardens swim together, fading at the edges into grainy, black and white checks.

At last, in the furthest corner of the garden, Sarah finds the perfect stick, lying pale and sanded, the kind of stick you would expect to find on a beach, beneath a privet hedge. 'Joshy,' she calls, half-running, half-skipping back along the gravel path, oblivious to the fact that it is still before nine on a Sunday morning. 'Fetch!' She hurls the stick, but Joshua has returned it almost before the words leave her mouth. She grabs one end and wrestles with him playfully. 'Dead, Joshy! Dead!' He opens his jaw. 'Good boy!'

Suddenly it's as if a decision has been made. Even before Catherine feels the pain in her head, or the hard, cool concrete pressing up against her bones, she is aware of it. Her daughter's childish, exuberant commands carry up from the garden, but already she doesn't seem to recognise the voice. She opens her eyes and blinks at the blue and white sky, her temples pound with pumping blood. Slowly, the nausea seeps away, leaving her completely numb.

She pulls herself into a sitting position, clenching her fists round the railings as if they were bars in a cell. The ten-year-old in the garden whirls her stick as high as she can up into the air. The yellow dog lurches forwards, trying to catch it as it helicopters down.

At that moment, Sarah looks back to the house. With a rush of relief she sees her mother sitting on the balcony, sunbathing. She waves.

Catherine goes to the door in her dressing gown, with yesterday's make-up smudged across her eyes and her hair in a mess. David looks away from the window panel and takes a step back. Silently, she lets him in.

'We need to talk,' he says awkwardly, following her upstairs.

'Well I didn't think you'd come for a fuck.' Catherine's heart is thumping like a landed fish but she sounds perfectly calm. She moves the Do Not Disturb sign they had stolen from the hotel in Jamaica from the bathroom to the study door. 'Take a seat.'

'Actually, I'd rather not.' They watch each other.

Catherine sits down, grasping her knees with her hands to stop them trembling. 'Say it then,' she bursts out at last.

'Say what?'

Catherine stares at her hands. 'You always were a coward,' she mutters, trying to ignore her heart's invisible, credulous, rush of hope.

'Were?'

She shrugs. David is scanning the bookshelves, almost absentmindedly, his dulled eyes flickering with recognition as they pass the spine of *The Frog-Lily*. 'Remember this?' He slides the volume off the shelf, allowing it to fall open at random as if he were about to recite.

'David, don't be cruel.'

'Sorry.' He replaces the book and sits down next to her on the sofa. 'I think we should . . .' he hesitates, almost gagging on the words. For a moment Catherine thinks he is going to propose. 'I think we should stop seeing each other.'

Suddenly the door flies open and Sarah stumbles in. She has been in the garden all morning and her jeans are green with grass stains. As she sees David the expression on her glowing, excited face freezes. Then she smiles at him with visible relief. 'When are we having lunch?' she asks.

Her mother has stood up. 'Have what you want, when you want, OK?' She marches Sarah back through the door and shuts her out.

Sarah sits at the top of the stairs, just below the study's thin pine door, staring down blindly into the empty hall, through the slit window and out into the street. Ready to vanish at a moment's notice, she waits for the argument to begin. But instead the sound of David's low talking voice mutters through, in short, uncomfortable bursts. It carries well enough, but she can't make out what he is saying. Her mother says hardly anything.

She tries to imagine that they are talking about work, and grafts words randomly to the music of their voices, like

a lyricist might but, every time she thinks she has understood, the rhythms and pace of altercation change and she
has to start again. It is a tiring, futile game. Shoes and ankles
blink on the pavement and shadows fade in and out as the
day clouds over.

Catherine stares across the length of the room and does not
see a thing. Her raw hands twist like lemon halves cupping
each knee. *It's funny,* she thinks, trying to breathe, *I have spent
weeks preparing for this. But now I am almost more profoundly
shocked than I would have been had he taken me by surprise, since
incredulity, the mind's automatic response, has been denied.*

David stares hopelessly out of the window, through the
branches of the pear tree three gardens down, waiting for the
silence to break.

*Though I have been in a kind of mourning for weeks and months
already, the thought that I might never see you again is taking my
breath away. I am sick but I can't feel a thing. All I can do is analyse my
own reaction. It is as if I were, to all intents and purposes, dead.*

'Say something, for God's sake.'

'What?'

'Speak to me.'

Catherine sits very still and grips her knees. 'I thought I
was.'

'I didn't hear a word. You didn't say anything.'

She reels. 'Is there anything I *could* say?'

'No.'

She speaks in a measured, almost considerate, voice. 'What
are you waiting for then?' A pigeon crashes free of the pear
tree and flies south. 'David?'

'I'm not waiting.' He hesitates, 'Are you all right?'

'What do you think?'

Now it's his turn to shrug. 'I didn't expect you to be so calm.'

Footsteps, slow, reluctant, deliberate, approach the door and Sarah races downstairs and switches the television on. The footsteps follow, as far as the hall. There is an undecided pause. Then the front door slams. Outside, David takes a deep breath and hurries away.

The house reverberates. Shudders echo from wall to wall and tremble through the floorboards into her naked feet. Catherine stands rooted to the spot and shakes, now, violently. Then she drops to her knees and crawls to bed.

Some time later Sarah knocks on the door with a lunch tray. Usually it shoulders open quite easily but today it has been pulled to and the tongue is in its groove. She puts the tray on the floor and grips the handle. She rattles the door in its frame and calls out. There is no reply. Crunching hungrily into a slice of cheese on toast, she wonders whether to phone her father. Orange grease slides down her chin and drips onto her favourite T-shirt. Maybe Mum's asleep, she decides, taking another bite. She carries the tray up to her room to finish, pulling out a pink silk eiderdown from the drawer beneath her bed to act as a picnic blanket. Arranging it into a neat, raspberry-coloured rectangle on the floor, she remembers how her mother had spotted it in amongst a heap of old clothes and knick-knacks in the garage one summer during a visit to Granny's.

'You can't throw this away, Mummy; Ma embroidered it herself,' her mother had said.

'I'm not throwing it away; I'm giving it to the church fête.'

'You can't do that.'

'Well what do I want with these old things?'

Not listening, Catherine had continued to rummage through the pile. 'And what about this?' She held up a dirty-looking toast rack. 'That's silver, you know.'

'Of course I know.'

'It's an heirloom, for God's sake.'

'Well take it then! I don't want it – I haven't got time to keep on polishing the thing, and I eat toast only in the morning. It comes straight out of the grill, nice and hot.' She winked at Sarah. 'That's how I like it.'

Catherine had rolled her eyes. 'I will. And Jesus, Mummy, don't go throwing anything else away without checking first with me, OK? It's madness.'

Her grandmother had looked sadly at what remained of the heap. 'I wasn't *throwing it away*.'

Sarah leans forward and buries her face in its puffy furrows, breathing in the smell of stale cigarettes, disinfectant, scent. Family dust.

Sarah hates Sunday afternoons, she decides, there is never anything good on telly – only racing cars and antiques – and never anything to do. She glances round her room at the bookshelves stacked with games and dolls as if in search of inspiration. Mum can't still be asleep, she thinks, opening the door a crack to listen for evidence of life. The house is quiet. She wanders downstairs and holds her breath, listening outside Catherine's room.

'Mum,' she whispers at last. 'Are you awake?'

Perhaps she's gone out. Sarah tiptoes into the study to see if her handbag is missing. There on the desk, on top of a pile of typing, lie her keys. The handbag sits like a lazy black cat on the chair by the telephone. She tries the bathroom door but it's locked too. 'Mum!' She is beginning to panic. 'Open the door, you're frightening me. Let me in!'

No one replies. 'I'm frightened, Mum. You're frightening me. Say something.'

Sarah leans against the corridor wall and listens. She looks at the second hand on her watch as it goes round and round. After a while it's time for *Jim'll Fix It*, so she creeps down to the drawing room.

Someone is knocking on the window. A key turns in the lock and the house shakes as the front door slams shut. Harry walks in.

'And what on earth do you think you're doing out of bed at this time?' He bends abruptly over the television and switches it off. Things have been busy at the office and Sarah hasn't seen him for a couple of weeks; he looks tired and grumpy, she thinks, deciding not to complain.

'Hi, Dad.'

'Come on then,' he sighs, holding out a hand for her. 'Bed.'

Sarah grabs it and pulls herself up off the sofa. 'What's going on?'

'I don't know.'

'Will you cheer her up?'

'I'll try. Come on, upstairs with you.'

Lying awake in bed Sarah listens to her mother and father moving around in the study below. Their voices grow louder and louder until she can hear individual words quite distinctly; then they drop back down to an almost comforting murmur. She doesn't mean to fall asleep, but suddenly she feels so tired. Rain starts up against the window.

Marion fumbled in her sleep for the alarm clock, gummed eyes groping its gently luminous face: 2.40 a.m. But the ringing did not stop, neither did it ring the way her alarm clock usually rang. Somewhere, a dog seemed to be barking. She removed the batteries, dropping them onto the floor with two sharp thuds. Jamie shifted.

'Who the hell's that?'

'What?' she said drowsily.

'Ringing?'

'My God!' She leapt out of bed and hurried downstairs. Ollie was whining at her from the other side of the door. The telephone seemed to be screaming for her, like Toby had, as a baby, waking for his night feed. She forced herself to walk the last few steps as an exercise in self-control. If the news was that bad, whoever it was would certainly wait.

'Hello?'

Atmospherics fuzzed in her ear.

'Hello?' There was definitely someone listening at the other end of the line. She held her breath. Minutes seemed to pass. Her heartbeat slowed, she began to shiver. The tiles in the kitchen were cold. Moonlight shone on the backs of the chairs. Suddenly the caller sighed, shattering the silence, and hung up. Relieved and disappointed, Marion released her grip. The dialling tone came on. The receiver seemed to grow heavier and heavier. She put it down and stared out of the window. It was a clear night, and shadows leaned out, like moats, from the feet of walls and hedges. Molehills loomed like pyramids on the silvered lawn.

'Everything all right?' asked Jamie as she slipped back into bed, his voice gravelly with sleep.

'Think so. Dead.' She shuddered. 'Wrong number, probably.'

'Someone else's disaster. Makes a change.' He rolled over to face her. 'God, you're icy cold. Come here.' Gradually their legs interlocked. The warm palm of his hand ran softly up and down her back.

Next door, Sarah also rolled over, wide awake. She listened to their murmuring voices and the muffled creak of the bed.

It is dark one moment, then suddenly it isn't, and somebody is ringing the doorbell. Sarah wakes up instantly, throws on her clothes and runs downstairs. The study door is open and her mother sits hunched on her chair, speaking into the phone.

'Yes. She's just come down,' she says, her voice half-swallowed. Tremulous. Extremely slow. 'Yes.' Very gradually she stretches out her arm to pass the receiver, and looks at her daughter. Deep, round, grey and purple rings sag beneath her swollen eyes and her cheeks are scarred with creases. The white of her arms is smudged with dried blood. Sarah takes the phone incredulously.

'Hello, Sarah, I'm Karen. I'm a friend of Mummy's.' The woman's voice is sensible and kind. Sarah wonders how she knows her name. 'She isn't feeling very well so we need you to be Mummy's legs and go and open the front door and let the ambulance men in. Are you listening?'

'Yes.'

'Good. Then come back to the phone. Do you understand?'

'OK.' Sarah puts the phone on the table and runs downstairs to open the door. The ambulance men on the doorstep say hello and check that they are at the right address, then they follow her into the house. She picks up the phone again.

'Are they there with you now, Sarah?'

'Yes.'

'They're going to take Mummy to hospital,' the woman says, 'but don't be frightened. She's OK. All right?'

'Yes,' says Sarah.

'Why don't you help her pack a few things she might want to have with her while she's there?'

'Yes.'

'Good. You're a very brave girl. I've phoned Daddy and he says he'll meet you at the hospital. You should go now. Goodbye.' Sarah puts the receiver on its hook and looks at the ambulance men who are half-walking, half-carrying her mother back across the carpet from the bathroom.

'She said I should pack—'

'Be quick,' says the man on the right.

'My handbag . . .' Catherine turns weakly to look over her shoulder as they huddle her through the door. Sarah picks it up and grabs the house keys and the nearest book she can find. Then she takes a carrier bag from the kitchen and crams into it a pair of jogging shoes, some socks and knickers and an 'I love Jamaica' T-shirt.

It is still quite dark in the back of the ambulance. Catherine lies on a stretcher with her eyes open, her swollen face shining grey with tears. Sarah sits towards the front, looking over the driving seat and out through the tinted window. 'Have you ever been in an ambulance before?' the driver asks.

She shakes her head and stares at a row of unfamiliar knobs and dials on the dashboard.

'Good,' he smiles. 'The less of these things you see the better. Shall we put the siren on?'

Sarah nods eagerly.

While Catherine has her stomach pumped, Sarah is sent to wait in the hospital stock room. Her father hasn't arrived yet and the nurses want her somewhere close by so they can keep an eye on her. It is a desolate, musty place with only one lightbulb hanging from the ceiling and no curtains for its narrow north-facing windows. A couple of rusty hospital beds with ancient, stained mattresses wait patiently to be brought out of retirement in case of emergency. Cardboard boxes full of variously sized bandages and toilet paper gather dust on the shelves. The walls are filthy and the windows covered with spider's webs. Paint has bubbled off the corners of the ceiling and flaked to the floor to be crushed into still more dust against the lino.

Sarah spots a comic rolled up between two of the boxes on a shelf she thinks she can reach by standing on the closest bed, but doesn't dare try to get it. Nurses pop in and out continually, fetching things. She decides to play I-spy solitaire to pass the time, beginning with the letter A, intending to work through to the end of the alphabet, but every time she looks round the room the comic's fading grey spiral catches her eye.

'Your dad's arrived, love. Come with me.' The door has opened without her noticing. Wiping her eyes with the back of her hand, she smiles guiltily at the nurse and jumps off the edge of the bed.

Harry stands with his back to the door in the middle of the

empty waiting room, shuffling from foot to foot impatiently;
he holds a small leather suitcase in one hand and seems to be
leaning forward, like an animal about to strain its leash. He has
always hated hospitals – the smell of them makes him gag –
and he hates his wife for making him come. Watching as he
twists round to greet her, Sarah catches his look like a punch
in the face. Reeling, she takes another step forward.

'Dad?'

'Darling.' The hatred evaporates. 'Are you OK?'

She nods. 'Are you?'

'Of course I am.' He smiles at her quickly. 'Shall we go?
The doctor says we can't see Mum until this evening.'

Sarah hesitates, looking back over her shoulder as if to
check with the nurse. 'OK.'

They walk in silence to the car, Sarah half-trotting to keep
up with him.

'Cheer up, Dad,' she says, looking up at his grim, determined face. 'It wasn't your fault.'

They climb into the car. Harry smiles bitterly through the
windscreen.

'Do you love me?'

Ben has gone to Cornwall for a long weekend. The weather forecast predicted showery intervals in the west and it took him forty minutes to pack: shorts, swimming trunks, jeans, an anorak – an outfit suitable for whatever occasion or situation he could possibly encounter in a quiet seaside village over the space of five days in August. So many clothes and books and shoes, in fact, that he gave up trying to cram them into his own suitcase and had to borrow mine. He was standing in the kitchen wondering what food to take for the drive, looking coy. Or rather, since he knew my answer, pretending to.

'Yeah, yeah. Only go, will you, I haven't got all day to spend hanging around on the doorstep waiting to kiss your prickly face goodbye,' I joked, in the manner of one who has heard it all before. We joke about anything.

'Say it then.'

'I love you.'

'Good.' He helped himself to an apple, ducking out of the kitchen to check one last time that he hadn't forgotten anything and suddenly, as if I had only just accepted the fact that

he really was going to leave, the sight of it, red as a cricket ball
in his outstretched hand, seemed full of poignancy. I wished
he wouldn't go. Or rather, since he had to, I wished he'd just
get on with it. I too had social promises to keep today.

'Goodbye,' I said, hustling him out of our bedroom and
along the corridor, but he made me go with him out to the
car. We couldn't remember where I had parked it, and wandered down the middle of the street looking left and right.

'But will you love me for ever?' he worried lightly, guiding
me back to safety as an ice-cream van sped by, nursery rhymes
blaring.

'I'll do anything you want,' came my extravagant reply.

'Will you?' For a moment he seemed satisfied. 'Why?'

'Because I love you.'

'Why?'

In so far as it is possible to shrug with a tennis racquet
hanging from your shoulder, I shrugged. 'Because I do,' I
said, already wishing I could have thought of a more imagi-
native response. There will always be some questions best left
unasked and this is one of them, even though we joke about
everything and nothing is kept sacred. Ben walked round to
unlock the car so I couldn't see if he was disappointed; he
adjusted the driving seat.

'Bye then, Shorty,' he teased, switching the ignition on
with one hand and unwinding the sunshine roof – as he calls
it – with the other. Last year, after months of dispute, I was
finally forced to accept the judgement of an independently
selected tape-measure and he will never let me forget the one
and three-quarter inches difference.

'Bye. Safe journey.'

Waving, he motored into the distance. A battered-looking electrician's van turned down the road and, once again, I was shocked by my emotional ambivalence. It's a kind of independence – a magnificent numbness I seem always to have felt. Sometimes I dare myself to imagine what it would be like if he drove away and never came back. How quickly would I learn to sleep in the middle of the bed? How easily would I forget his pin number, his birthday, the colour of his lips when he wakes up, too hot, in the morning?

I went back inside and cleared away breakfast, trying to think instead of good things: the way he paces round his car at night, inspecting the locks; the way he washes, religiously, every morning but forgets to clean his teeth until just before lunch. How he can spend a quarter of an hour in the supermarket looking for the right kind of bacon – rindless, back, unsmoked – when there it is in front of him all the time, but he doesn't like it in a floppy packet, only a plastic box will do. I love it that everything goes right for him, down to the smallest detail, sometimes by luck and sometimes simply because he wills it to. I get too much pleasure from seeing him have what he wants.

Outside it is bright and much too hot. I cross to the shady side of the street, where three women with paper fans and bulging carrier bags stand chatting by an open front door, complaining about the heat, the price of cucumbers, their kids. Their loose-necked shirts, untucked, with the sleeves rolled up above the elbow, are damp with sweat. The sky is hazy with pollution. I am thinking of Ben and wishing I'd thought of something better than 'because I do' to say.

'*Why do you love me?*'

'*Because you're the most beautiful person I have ever met.*'

He said that once. We were on holiday, waiting after dark by the side of the road for a bus. It was like being given a crown. Hammered out of the palest gold and set with diamonds. Heavy, and rather frightening. I kept very still, sitting up straight, and watched the gold that shone from it rest on the dusty pavement where we sat, lighting up the crumbs and the dust and the footprints and a few little insects who were taking away the pieces of our sandwich that had dropped. Other light-loving insects soon found their way into its beam, moths especially. It lit up the pavement far away, where people were waiting for the bus, Mexicans and perhaps a few more tourists like us, and it was as if I had never properly seen them, or any-one, before, only now: the dark figures, men and bulky women watching over their luggage and children, lit up on one side through the window of the sandwich bar, and then again, only differently, by me. All the shadows faced away from me, and all the light pointed in my direction. I had the crown on my head and felt like the most beautiful person Ben had ever met.

Afterwards the coach driver came out of the sandwich bar and climbed up into his cabin and everyone formed a more or less orderly line, waiting to be let on. We followed the Pacific coast down towards the Guatamalan border at Tapachula. I sat by the window and Ben rested his head on my shoulder, falling asleep. I held myself straight, looking out of the window, beneath the double weight of his head, now fully relaxed and swollen to its utmost heaviness with sleep, and the crown I wore. And somewhere at the end of the road the flat coastal plains would be interrupted by volcanoes, the first I had seen, and we would get off the bus and wait for the next connection

to take us to Guatemala City where, perhaps, he might meet
another person, someone more beautiful than me.

Guatemala City exists on the brink of a cholera epidemic. We
went everywhere with at least one bottle of mineral water in
our shoulder bag and watched for vomiting and milky diar-
rhoea. We wandered into a half-bombed-out, or perhaps just
half-constructed, multi-storey car park in the hope that it
would lead, as multi-storey car parks often do at home, to a
land of supermarkets, sleeping policemen and freshly painted
double yellow lines. Five floors up and we emerged, instead,
in the middle of a vast concrete playing field, littered with
broken glass and polythene.

'Let's go back.' Ben dribbled an abandoned football
slowly – it was the middle of the day and very hot – towards
an imaginary goal. Volcanoes triangled at the edges of the city
grid, behind the smog, one of them releasing little black puffs
of smoke into the cloudless sky. I felt suddenly uneasy, vulnerable and a long way from the nearest trustworthy soldier,
the nearest hospital. Our mineral water was running out.

Back at the hotel we showered, one by one, with our
mouths and even our eyes shut tight against contamination.
We flopped down on the bed and waited to be ill. We were
frightening ourselves. I think we were frightening ourselves
on purpose, the way people do when they have something to
prove but not patience enough to wait at home for an appropriately testing situation. It was a kind of trial by anxiety, as
though if we could come through this without falling out or
getting me pregnant then there could be nothing left for ordinary life to throw at us that we wouldn't survive.

Our money was running out as well. I had taken off my crown and given it to the proprietor to guard, along with my camera, our passports, the last few travellers cheques. Instead of a lock and key our room had a Christmas cracker padlock, opened by a slip of aluminium one step more sophisticated than a hairpin. The walls were tongue and groove, painted pink, like raspberry ice-cream, and at night we dropped off to sleep to the gnawing of rats. But we had brought our own mosquito net and fixed its corners precariously to a nail and three more-or-less opportune splinters in the wall. Inside we were safe from rats and disease and everything.

Our guide book failed to mention the French boulangerie behind the Terminal Occidente. For nearly an hour we watched the steady trickle of baguettes, wrapped up comfortably in yellow wax paper, progressing down the street. We followed the trail, the way you follow a parade of ants to find its nest. Ben made a note of the address and opening times, part of the daydream that we would give up on England and travel the world together writing niche guide books for people who wish they could have stayed at home. We turned our bread into tomato sandwiches and set off for the Parque La Libertad on the edge of the city, a popular tourist destination 'carved into the sides of a dead volcano'.

Two men eyed us hungrily on the bus but I had forgotten them by the time we arrived and pulled Ben in the direction of a reconstructed Mayan pyramid.

'Hold on,' he called me back.

'Why?' I was about to make a fuss.

'Shut up!' he whispered. Slowly our bus load broke into smaller groups and filtered down the hillside out of sight.

'What's going on?'

'Nothing.' He paused, looking thoughtfully into the middle distance. 'I just want to wait here for a while.'

I turned my back on him and counted out small change for a Coke. The woman in the snack bar smiled at me sympathetically as she cracked off the bottle lid, tipping its contents into a plastic cup. She thought we were having a fight and that was to let me know whose side she took.

'OK, then. Let's go.' He steered away from the main avenue, keeping us in full view of the car park.

'What's wrong?' I asked again.

'Nothing,' he repeated, squeezing my hand in reassurance. We gazed at another aerial view of the city, its streets laid out like a sheet of graph paper. A family of Europeans hurried up the path towards us and as they came closer we could tell that something awful had happened.

'Don't go down there!' they pointed, all talking at once in voices jerky with adrenaline. They were German, or Dutch. I remembered envying the daughter's platinum blonde hair on the bus.

'We were robbed. They have a gun. Come with us, it isn't safe here,' said the father.

The daughter was crying in fits and starts. 'He touched me, here,' she covered the zip of her khaki shorts and shuddered, catching her breath in another violent sob.

'Are you all right? Is there anything we can do?' I asked.

'They got my camera. All our money,' the father shouted back over his shoulder. They marched uncertainly to the bus stop.

'Thanks for the warning,' I called after them. Ben looked

away for a moment, chewing his lip, and then it was my turn
to shake. 'How did you know?'

He shrugged. At the bus stop he made me give them
money for the journey home. The crown was back on my
head and heavier than before, less comfortable. I did everything he said without question for the rest of the week.

In the delicatessen – the best place round here, says Mum, to
go for quality, fresh ingredients – there is a queue. Shop keep-
ers dropping in early to avoid the lunchtime rush, ladies with
dinner parties to arrange picking up authentic cheese, and a
well-dressed young woman I think I recognise. Maybe we
were at school together, though I don't remember her name.
There is certainly something familiar about her face and the
way she holds the strap of her elegant black leather bag against
her shoulder. I take a basket and squeeze through to the back
room looking for flour. It smells of cinnamon and cardboard
boxes. This is where I used to come for emergency puddings
when David was round.

Piling up ingredients on top of the salami counter, I notice
her again, at the front of the queue by now. Her hand is stuck
between the pages of a recipe book. One of the cheese assis-
tants offers his help and she proceeds to read out aloud a list of
ingredients. She does not move from her place, by the Gor-
gonzola, as he rushes from shelf to shelf. She too is making a
chocolate cake, and I am suddenly sick with the thought that,
one day, Ben might meet her and see how much more beautiful than me she is. And I wonder if Mum ever felt like this
about the possibility of losing David.

Catherine lies still in the shadowy room, remembering things. She is trying to understand exactly how it is that she comes to be lying here, in such a state, but every explanation seems to require an explanation of its own so, in the end, she has just decided to give up and start, from fresh as it were, at the beginning. In hospital. A cleaning trolley rattles along the corridor outside. There is a pause, a silence interrupted by a knock on the door.

'Go away.'

She is a baby, lying on her back in the crib though, surely, this can't be the hospital she was born in. She is older than that; she is bored. Outside the shriek of passing ambulances doesn't frighten her, but something isn't right, isn't comfortable. The blankets have not been tucked under properly. Air is getting in, making her almost cold. There's too much space. If she moves she thinks she might fall out. She wishes someone warm would come and hold her. She still misses the beating of her mother's heart. The ceiling is like an endless, dirty white sky. Occasionally it trembles, and particles of dust float down.

There is another silence, followed by another knock and the rattle of keys.

'I said go away.' The door swings open. 'Leave me alone.' She is a girl again, four years old and folded into the cubby-hole, blinking at the light on her grandmother's face.

Ma holds out a hand and crouches. 'Come on, Cathy.' She almost whispers, talking to her the way you would talk to a timid animal. They stare at each other.

'Oh, I'm sorry. I didn't know you were here.' The chambermaid casts a professional eye about the room to check that everything, or as much as can be expected, is in order. 'Shall I do the bed?'

'No thank you.' Catherine has turned her head away and stares at the curtains as they suck in and out. The window is a bending square of orange light.

'Tomorrow then.'

She must have been happy living in her grandmother's house. The day they were supposed to leave she went into hiding.

She had planned it in advance, of course, surreptitiously redistributing the bed linen in the cubby-hole at the bottom of the dresser to make a lair. Vexed by the geometrical conundrum of how to fit their accumulated possessions into one small trunk and three packing cases, none of the grown-ups had noticed her slip downstairs. She took off her shoes and opened the cubby-hole door, turning its round brass knob to release the secret tongue inside. She had already worked out the best way to sit, with her knees drawn up as far as her chin, and crept in head first, reaching out to grab the sandals and pull the door shut after her. She fiddled the tongue back into its wooden groove and waited. And waited. Every minute she heard the long hand on the kitchen clock click forwards a notch, and tried to amuse herself by counting the sixty imaginary seconds in between.

Ma swished in, flop-flopping in her house shoes, her long skirt brushing against the dresser as she passed, and turned the water on. Catherine squinted through a chink in the wooden door to discover what her grandmother was doing. She heard the little stool bump over the tiles, then Ma's skirt swishing as she stepped up on to it to reach the cupboard. Making tea by the sound of things.

She didn't want them to leave either, Catherine had heard her say so. 'Coventry seems a very long way away.' They were to go by train, which her stepfather spoke of with excitement, as if it were something she was meant to look forward to. Something they must not miss. She was unimpressed. Did he think she had never seen a train before? Did he think she was a baby? She frowned at the thought of him. Why couldn't he go to Coventry on his own and just come round for tea, as he had before the wedding?

Another pair of footsteps approached the kitchen, heel-toe heel-toe, businesslike, bruising the hall's wooden floorboards, clattering on the tiles. An aunt, she guessed, holding her breath.

'Have you seen Cathy, Ma? Sheila's not halfway through the packing and her taxi's due any minute.' The baby cooed and Catherine's aunt sat down, creaking into a chair. 'That's better,' she sighed.

'Will they have time for a cup of tea?'

'I doubt it. Ted's still trying to get the cases shut and Sheila can't find her fountain pen and swears she won't get on the train without it. Not to mention Cathy.' She laughed. 'She's probably hiding somewhere, poor thing.'

'She doesn't want to go,' said Ma. Water spat and hissed as she hoiked the kettle off the stove.

'I know we'll miss them,' said Catherine's aunt confidingly, 'but it'll be a relief when they've gone and we can have space to breathe.'

Ma tutted. 'Space to breathe and plenty of worry to fill it with. Here, let me.' Marion was passed, gurgling, across the kitchen table to be bounced by her grandmother. 'She's going to miss the baby.'

Curled at the bottom of the dresser, Catherine wondered whether to give herself up. She peered through the crack again, keeping her head as still as possible, focusing. A slice of the table, and above it Ma's white sleeve with a bit of Mari's hair, the peppermint wall going up and up and up. It was like that game her mother had taught them at school, when you show only a little bit of the picture at a time.

The Citroën slowed to a stop and reversed abruptly into a parking bay, its windscreen wipers freezing mid-swing. A box of soft centres, three video tapes and a large bouquet – roses, mallow and delphiniums from the garden, their long stems wrapped in wads of damp tissue paper, clingfilm and a rubber band – slid back on the passenger seat. Marion had not been to visit her aunt for several weeks.

St Margaret's was dying, like many of its patients, from the inside out. It lay on the outskirts of Oswold, a genteel market town on the edge of the moors, about an hour's drive from the farmhouse. Enclosed by pebble-dashed prefabs and a network of immaculately tarmacked paths, the original building – a gloomy, red-brick purpose-built asylum – sulked with an air of offended grandeur. Its serried windows had been boarded up for years, but the surrounding sprawl received fresh coats of paint, sympathetic inter-departmental signposting, a flourish of neatly pruned herbaceous borders and prospered. Marion pulled up her jacket collar over her head and ran for it.

In the lobby a disconsolate nurse waited for the rain to let

up, interrupting her habitual inspection of the ward's com-
memorative plaque, Dr John Hurley's bronze and the dust in
the vase of silk chrysanthemums to welcome the newcomer.
Marion smiled and rolled her eyes. 'Miserable weather!'
Prerecorded laughter echoed along the corridor. In the day
room, outpatients and residents, cosily slumped round teacup-
littered coffee tables, waited for lunch. They ignored the
sitcom. One or two made conversation, looking up as Marion
passed. Matron, an elegant, young Glaswegian, summoned
her into a corner.

'You've not come at the best time, Mrs Heath. She's just
had her medication. She'll be dropping off to sleep.'

Marion looked at her watch. 11.30.

'Could you come back in a couple of hours?'

'Not really. How is she?'

'We had a bit of a cold last week. Better now.' She caught
the eye of a passing nurse and nodded minutely towards the
steamed-up windows. 'It's so stuffy in here. Come on then,
I'll take you in.' As she bustled off towards the private rooms,
Marion wondered again what on earth attracted this woman
to geriatric care.

Sheila lay curled up on her side, facing the television. The
volume had been turned off and an advert for washing powder flickered silently in the curtained gloom. The bedclothes
failed to disguise how thin she had become.

'Mrs Hardcastle, you've a visitor.' Slowly, the body moved.
The head turned. Her face had changed too; her bones had
risen to the surface. Suddenly she looked as though she might
have, once, been beautiful. A trick of the light. Her frizzy
white hair had been cut.

'Sheila . . .' Marion leaned over the bed and kissed her cold, wet, papery cheek.

'Catherine,' she rasped. 'How lovely.'

'No, Aunt. It's me.' No look of confusion spread across the old woman's face, she had already forgotten. The door clicked sensitively behind them.

'Marion. What a relief. I thought you were never coming back. Tell me, is today Sunday?'

'Tuesday.'

'Tuesday . . .' She lifted a trembling finger, as if about to bless. 'Turn it off, will you. And help me with these pillows.' Pausing to catch her breath, she continued, 'Are those for me? How lovely. No dear, I can't smell a thing.'

Marion withdrew the flowers. 'They're from the garden. Jamie sends his love. And Sarah, she's come to stay for a while. I'll bring her with me, next time, if you like.'

'How lovely. That would be nice.' She scratched at the back of her hand. 'Is this a wart do you think?'

Marion bent to examine it more closely. The bump was pea-sized and scaly with dead skin. 'I'm afraid it is.'

'How horrible,' she said, scratching at it again, vindictively.

'I'll buy it off you.' The younger woman reached for her handbag, shocked that, with the rest of her body so eaten by illness and old age, her aunt should be troubled by something as cosmetic as a wart. 'How much do you want for it?'

'Fifty pence?'

'Done.' The purse clicked open and Marion pinched out a coin and put it carefully on the bedspread.

Sheila squeezed it into her palm. 'Abracadabra,' she said, smiling like a girl. 'I hope it goes.'

'Oh it will.' Marion paused. 'I'm sorry it's been so long. I've been very busy.'

'Nonsense. Don't be. I'm glad you've gone back to teaching – they're so charming at that age.'

'Teaching?' For a moment Marion thought she must have heard wrong.

'When the classroom goes completely quiet . . . only the sound of pencils scribbling in exercise books and you can actually feel the concentration . . . Those were the happiest days of my life, you know.'

Perching on the edge of the bed, Marion reached out to cover her aunt's clammy hand with her own.

'Have you brought me any cigarettes?'

'I'm sorry. You know they're not allowed.'

Sheila's face tightened with disappointment. She thought about smoking only when visitors came. It was so cruel.

'I'm sorry, Aunt,' said Marion again.

'Tell Catherine I want to see her. The minute she gets in. It's urgent.'

'How are you feeling?'

Sheila closed her eyes and sighed. 'Deliciously drowsy.'

'Shall I leave you to sleep?'

'You've only just arrived. All that way. Tell Catherine to wake me up. I don't mind. As soon as she comes in. Ted's going away, you see, and I want her to be there to say goodbye.'

Marion squeezed her hand. 'Uncle Ted's dead, Sheila. You're in a muddle. Why not have a sleep?'

'I'm deliciously drowsy.'

'I'll come again soon,' she backed out, guilty, gentle, 'I promise.'

'Night then.'

'Good night.' She closed the door quietly and stood for a minute outside, staring in through its porthole as the old woman inched herself back onto her side. Her left hand groped for something on the bedside table. The television screen quietly exploded into colour.

'Anything happen while I was gone?'

Jamie smiled mysteriously and pulled his wife into his arms. 'Anyone would think you'd been away for a month, not a morning.' He gave her a kiss. 'I've been volunteered to help Sarah and her little friend build a dam. Harry phoned – nothing urgent, just wanted to chat – and there was another dead call. That's it. How's your aunt?'

'Very bad. She's losing it. We should have had her come and live here rather than stay in that hospital. God it's a depressing place.' Marion's eyes scanned the kitchen. 'She thought I'd gone back to school.' She paused. 'Don't say it.'

'Maybe you should.' They spoke simultaneously.

'Maybe you should,' he repeated. 'It's going to feel very quiet here when Sarah goes. You'll need something to do.'

She examined the weave of his shirt, the cornflower blue threads crisscrossing with the white. 'What did Harry say?'

'Oh, nothing about that.'

'Has he heard from Catherine yet?'

'No. He wants to come up next weekend. OK?'

Marion shrugged, pushing herself away from his broad chest almost petulantly. 'I wish he could just leave her here forever.'

Ted sat up straight at the kitchen table, drumming his fingers. His mother-in-law's house was still and silent. Outside, boys were playing in the street. He could hear them running, the sharp, hollow thuds of their kicking boots, the fat ball scuffing the road, and wanted to join in. He had played a fair bit of football during the war: four- or-five-a-side and other impromptu variations. He'd been good in defence, but that was years ago. The long hand of the kitchen clock edged backwards in preparation for the next lost minute. He held his breath. It clicked.

Surely Ma should be back by now, or one of Sheila's sisters? The drumming grew louder, clumsy as his fingers tired. He had had the same old marching chant going round and round in his head for days, like a stuck record. *Had a good job and I LEFT, serves me jolly well RIGHT, had a good job and I LEFT.* A football skittered into the wall beneath the front-room window and his fingers skipped a beat. He reached the yard in a matter of seconds, threw himself against the fence and came to shivering, gulping for air. He lit a cigarette.

'Pathetic,' he said out loud. 'Grow up!'

Back in the kitchen he sat down again, smoked a second fag.

A third. Slowly his hand grew calm, his breathing more regular, and now he wasn't scared any more, just angry. They shouldn't have left him alone in the house like this, with nothing but a child for company, they should have known he wasn't up to it. He was getting worse, not better. The doctor was a fool. He stood, scraping the chair, and remembered Ma's instruction to let Cathy sleep as long as possible. He crept up the narrow stairs to their room and cautiously pushed the door open.

She had been grumpy after lunch, and tired. Sheila made her a nest in the middle of their bed. Surrounded like that, with the pillows and blankets scrunched up all around for walls and her favourite eiderdown on top to keep her warm, she looked even smaller than usual. Fragile. She was frightened of beds and still slept in the cot even though she was nearly five and getting too big for it. Soon it would be Marion's turn. Bending over, he listened carefully to the shallow, childish breaths, swallowing her warm, milky smell with a pang of envy. This was the first time he had been alone with her in the house. Gingerly he sat on the edge of the mattress and lifted a hand to stroke her hair.

'Cathy,' he whispered, shaking her shoulder gently. 'Cathy, wake up, princess.' The eyes blinked open reluctantly and he watched as a confused, anxious expression took the place of sleepiness. 'Hello, baby,' he whispered, bending to kiss her cheek. Catherine turned, frowning. 'Did you sleep well?'

She sat up, kicking away the pink eiderdown, and crossed her legs. 'Where's Mummy?'

'Still teaching, princess. And Grandma's at the shops.'

Her round chin puckered and the bottom lip began to shake. 'When will they be back?'

'I don't know, princess, but don't cry. There's a good girl.'
Why couldn't she be pleased to see him? He was panicking
already. 'You go back to sleep. There, there.'

'What time is it?' She rubbed her eyes.

'I don't know, princess. Mummy'll be home soon. Or
Grandma.'

'I'm thirsty.'

'Let's go downstairs and get a drink. Come on, I'll carry
you.' He stuck out his neck, waiting for her to stretch out her
skinny arms and grab hold.

'There's a cup in my Auntie Grace's room.' She didn't
move.

'Let's go downstairs.'

'No. I don't want to.'

'But I've got something to show you,' he lied coaxingly.
The little girl's eyes brightened with curiosity.

'What is it?'

'Wait and see.'

She shuffled away from him across the mattress and swung
her legs over the edge. The bare feet dangled. 'Have you got
my shoes?'

'I'll carry you,' he offered a second time, wanting to feel
her weight in his arms, her warmth, but not yet daring to lift
her up without permission.

'I want my shoes.'

Ted bent down to look under the bed, the blood rushing to
his brain. 'Where are they?'

'I don't know.' Again the lips wobbled and the puckered
chin threatened tears.

Dizzy, he walked round to look on the other side, for the

first time noticing the way the squares in the carpet made a
sequence of yellow and rose-pink swastikas. 'Why don't I
carry you down? That way you won't need them.'

'I do need them,' she insisted, still not moving from the bed.

He was beginning to sweat again. There were swastikas
everywhere now, crooked crosses reaching out from the window frame, the bedstead, the panels in the door. He opened
the wardrobe, desperately rummaged through the chest of
drawers, pulled at the curtains. 'There they are!'

They walked downstairs separately. The boys outside still
knocked their football around.

Catherine followed her stepfather into the kitchen and
allowed herself to be lifted, standing, onto the table, shoes and
all. 'What is it?' she said, again and again.

'I'll show you,' he answered, racking his brain. He moved a
chair to one side and took a few steps back. 'I'm going to
teach you how to fly.'

Catherine looked at him with amazement. 'Really?'

He nodded.

'How?'

'All you have to do is jump. Don't worry, I'll catch you.' He
held out his arms encouragingly.

Catherine gazed down at his brown Oxfords suspiciously.
They seemed an awfully long way off.

'Come on, Cathy. It's fun. Imagine you're a spitfire. Don't
be scared. I'll catch you.' He wiggled his fingers like a clown,
beckoning her, and smiled in reassurance.

She froze. 'I don't want to.'

'Don't look down,' he coaxed. 'Just shut your eyes and
jump!'

'I can't,' she said in a quiet voice, closing one eye at a time. A dizzying sickness rose from her stomach and she started to sway.

'That's right, princess. Now, on the count of three.'

She opened her eyes again as if to check he was still there.

'You've got to trust me, Cathy. You'll like it. I promise. Shut them again.' He paused. 'Are you ready now?'

She nodded reluctantly.

'One . . . Two . . . Three . . .'

Catherine took a deep breath, leapt. And as she launched herself Ted stepped back, dropping his arms to his sides. She smacked heavily into the floor and crumpled.

'That'll teach you,' he said, picking her up swiftly. 'No broken bones.'

He kissed her forehead and patted her hair coldly. 'Come on, princess. It was only a bit of fun. Don't cry.'

Catherine raised her head from the bathroom floor, focusing on the grid of shiny green tiles. A short, dark pubic hair – not one of mine, she thought – lay trapped in the grouting not six inches away from her mouth, fluttering as she breathed in and out. It was unhygienic. She would complain. She had paid good money to stay here. Couldn't anything just be right?

Drizzle needled the surface of the pool, churned mud shone in the grey light, and the marsh grass at the bottom of the field stood still. Protected by oversized hand-me-down anoraks and hats, Sarah and George had nevertheless managed to get themselves soaked to the skin. Thanks to well-fitting wellington boots, their feet were dry, but cold. Their trousers were spattered with dissolving globs of mud. Sarah's hair dangled in rat's tails at the nape of her neck; milky drops welled at the ends and, falling off, seeped hungrily into her shoulders. She shivered with enjoyment. George clomped off to find more stones.

The barricade was now almost complete and already the pool seemed wider. Less water ran down the small waterfall below the bridge. The trickle sounded quieter.

'Imagine if it gets deep enough to swim in,' said George, returning with a rough, sandy-coloured slab in each hand.

Sarah kicked the chocolate brown water. 'Yuk!'

George kicked back and they laughed as fresh splashes streaked across the front of her anorak. Grinning, he let go of the stones, plunged his hands into the murk and groped around, drawing up two fistfuls of sloppy mud. Sarah shrieked and ran to the bank for safety. 'No way! Pax. PAX.'

He squeezed the slime between his fingers and watched with delight as thick, glistening mud-worms slithered free, broke off and slapped back into the water, their dark stains swirling downstream.

'I'm going to find some leaves to block the gaps.' Sarah sashayed back towards the house.

Marion leaned on the windowsill, pressing her forehead against the chilly, rain-dashed pane. A pewter sky bellied in every raindrop. Close up like this all she could see was a universe of very large pearls, briefly suspended against the glass. Trees and fields slithered to the fringes of each watery globe and disappeared.

The boiler sang. Steaming water muttered into the bathtub. She seemed to spend most of her time in the bath these days. Outside, Sarah danced into view. She had taken off her hat, and its bowl was now half-filled with leaves and grass. Every few steps she stooped to grab another fistful, pressing it in firmly, leaving a path of dropped and discarded greenery as she trailed back towards the stream. Sliding open the window, Marion leaned out to call to her but Sarah ducked for another handful of grass, and disappeared behind the holly hedge. The greeting faded on her lips. A shock of cold air prickled her scalp.

'Shh,' said Jamie, standing up to his shins in mud at the edge of the pool. Sarah and George gazed at him and froze like statues. The hush of rain grew louder. The stream tinkled monotonously.

'Why?' George burst out after a minute of silence.

'We've got to listen for chinks.' He looked at the barricade. 'It's no good you just fumbling away underwater, stuffing bits of the garden into any old crack. You've got to be methodical. Listen first and discover where the holes are.' He cleared his throat.

They paddled closer to the dam and bowed over it intently.

'There!' cried Jamie suddenly, pointing into the water. 'A hole! Can you hear it?'

'No.'

'What? Are you deaf or something?'

'No!' they chorused. A crow beat past overhead. George fixed the imaginary hole and they listened again, Sarah crouching so low above the water that he was momentarily distracted by the temptation to push her in.

'I can hear something, I think.'

'Where?' Jamie cupped his ear and managed not to smile.

Marion slipped lower into the bath, stretching one foot to turn the hot tap on again, drowning out the voices that drifted up from the stream. She had left the window open. A breeze caressed her burning face while her arms and legs tingled in the near scalding water as it crept invisibly up her back. Particles of steam caught in the shroud of her hair. She felt her face glow. She was two weeks late. She relaxed her arms, watching them surface like a pair of sandbanks, and let her mind go blank.

The dam was finished. They rummaged around in Jamie's gardening shed, found a stash of bamboos and took one, breaking it in three. Along a line mysteriously selected by George as unlikely to be trampled by the cows, they pushed their markers into the mud and stepped back from the water's edge like scientists watching a new experiment begin.

If only she could travel back in time. Ten years, even five, would be enough. Three would do it. Catherine stared at herself in the mirror and pulled a face. Why couldn't they get proper, decent lighting in here? And why did the bathroom have to be so green? No wonder she looked ill. If only she could have her mirror from home she would be happy, she was sure. It wasn't much to ask for. A pony. A piano. Those were the years; she remembered them. Awful. Year after year of wanting *things*. Little things, which would have made all the difference then. A ribbon. A lollipop.

Catherine bit her tongue and blinked. It was her birthday and she mustn't cry. She gulped with disappointment.

'We know it isn't exactly what you wanted,' her mother was saying lamely, 'but your father and I thought it would be better to learn on this to begin with.' Stepfather, Catherine corrected silently. Sheila lifted the birthday present out of its debris of re-used wrapping paper and offered it to her daughter.

'Come on, Cathy,' said Ted. 'Don't upset Mummy. It took her a long time to make.' Catherine flashed him a look of resentment. This was all his doing, she knew.

'Cathy, it's only until we can afford a real piano. I'm sorry. We just haven't got the money this year.' Again her mother pushed the yard-long strip of wood towards her. Catherine looked down at the painted-on keyboard and wanted to cry. Apart from the letters, written in the middle of every note, it looked just like the real thing. A narrow, V-shaped groove had been chiselled lovingly between each of the keys and several layers of nail-varnish enamelled their black and white. Her mother had even written 'Bechstein' in yellow poster paint at the top.

'But it doesn't make a noise,' she burst out, bitterly. Everything about their life in Coventry had this air of unreality to it. The house, brand new and bought by her grandfather as an investment, which her parents occupied with eternal gratitude, living each day as if they had just twenty-four hours to pack up their belongings and go. School, where her mother, as a teacher-parent anticipating charges of favouritism, picked on her daily and where her classmates regarded her with suspicion. Every week was identical to the one before, right down to what they listened to on the radio, what they ate. Sausages for tea on Mondays to cheer her up, fish on Fridays, beef on Sundays after church. Saturdays were always special, chicken days, and she would be allowed to stay up half an hour longer too. After pudding she would fetch the wishbone from the airing cupboard and pull for it with Ted. He had thicker fingers than her and almost always won.

Sheila stared at her handiwork and puffed on a cigarette with obvious irritation. She couldn't see what all the fuss was about: it seemed a very good idea to her. This way, at least, they would all be spared the agony of having to listen to her practising. And when she grew bored of it they could just throw the thing away. 'Sometimes you can be a very selfish and hurtful little girl,' she said, gripping the edge of the wood with both hands as if about to tear it in half. 'You don't deserve a real piano.'

'Hold on!' said Ted, touching his wife's arm. '"Doesn't make a noise", did you say?' He looked incredulously at his stepdaughter. 'It's a piano. Of course it makes a noise.'

'No, it doesn't.'

'Yes it does. Sheila, put the Bechstein on the table, would you please. Careful! We don't want it going out of tune!'

'It couldn't go out of tune if it wanted to,' said Catherine. 'Listen,' and she jabbed her finger into the middle C. A proper father would have given her a real piano.

'La!' sang Ted.

Catherine looked at him with astonishment, then prodded the note again.

'La,' he repeated brusquely, his handsome face distorted in a parody of musical concentration. Catherine's finger hovered above the keyboard as she battled to control her urge to laugh.

Sheila looked on and held her breath. He had been with them five years now but Cathy was still difficult about it. In fact, she was difficult about a lot of things. 'She'll turn out to be a right troublemaker when she's older if you don't look out,' Ma had warned at Christmas. 'She's too clever for her own good. She needs taking in hand. Now. Before it's too late.'

Ted continued to stare at the piano, determined not to miss a note and steadfastly refusing to meet Catherine's eye.

He knew her well enough now to guess that she would try to catch him out. It was hard to imagine they had anything in common, but as a child he would have done exactly the same. The silence grew heavier as Catherine considered the possibilities. At last she stretched out both her index fingers and pressed the lowest and the highest available notes in alternation.

'Lo la lo la,' Ted sang simultaneously, stretching from bass to a shrill falsetto. She hesitated, then began again, her fingers moving more quickly up and down at both ends of the keyboard.

Her stepfather inhaled deeply. 'Lolalolalolalolalo,' he sang, his voice growing quieter and quieter as the breath ran out.

Catherine watched his face turn red. Maybe she could make him have a heart attack.

'Lolalolalo.' The voice was little more than a whisper now, and he mouthed hopelessly out of rhythm. For a moment she considered letting him off.

'Lo la lo,' he rasped, as Sheila suddenly snatched the piano out of her daughter's reach.

'ENOUGH!'

And Ted drew breath.

'Catherine, to your room.'

Catherine blinked at her mother, ashamed and triumphant.

'At once.'

The door swung open, brushing across a pile of letters, fly-ers and other junk mail. So she hadn't come back. The house seemed to resonate like an empty cell. Harry shook the rain from his shoes, flicked his hands dry and turned off the burglar alarm. He stamped on the mat and leafed through the post, sorting it according to apparent importance. There didn't seem to be any bills, for once – just a load of adverts from the estate agents and a statement from the building society in his name, which he stuffed into the pocket of his sodden jacket. He thought he'd given them his change of address. *Change of address!* He snorted. A sudden feeling of resentment flooded up from his fingertips as he shouldered into the drawing room, slapping down the post on top of the grand piano. That would annoy her; she hated to see its shiny black surface treated as a shelf. A jigsaw puzzle waited on the table, incomplete, and an old newspaper lay folded on the rug in front of the television. He didn't remember having seen it there last time.

In the kitchen he found a coffee mug half full of thick, dusty, blue-green mould. Three black ants scurried across the sideboard and he wondered whether or not to squash them.

He certainly felt in the mood for killing something, but the
thought of an infestation appealed to his inexplicable, unde-
niable desire for vengeance. He brought his thumb down
sharply over the body of the leading ant and watched the
indifferent survivors escape, weaving their way up the wall
between invisible obstacles. Then he hurried upstairs, deep
into the smell of her perfume. He checked the rest of the
house. Everything seemed to be all right.

'And how long has your wife been missing?'

Harry stared at the tip of the constable's poised ballpoint.
'About three weeks.'

It started to write, a firm vertical down-stroke, then
stopped again, abruptly. 'Can you be more exact?' He spoke
with businesslike sensitivity.

'Sorry.' He opened his diary and flicked back. Meetings
with clients. Deadlines. Theatre tickets booked, cancelled,
booked again. An interminable lunch with the contractors –
he remembered *that* – board meetings. 'She discharged herself
from hospital on the twenty-fifth. No one has seen or heard
from her since.'

'Is she in a vulnerable medical condition? Or had she, perhaps, received bad news with regard to her physical well-
being?'

'Ill, you mean? No. She took an overdose.'

The constable studied Catherine's photograph. Sarah had
taken it with the Polaroid they'd given her. A birthday present.
She was sitting on the sofa downstairs, her hands on her
knees, leaning forward slightly. She had painted her nails a soft
chestnut red. It was a formal pose. Next to her, Sarah's cake –

chocolate, its ten pink candles already burned three-quarters down, relit for the umpteenth time – glowed out of focus, unbalancing the whole composition.

'No, don't take us together, darling,' she had joked, shooting an almost spitefully seductive glance at Harry, 'or we'll have to cut the pictures in half.'

It won't come out well in black and white, he thought.

Physiognomy turned out not to lie within the constable's field of special ability. 'And is she, um, prone to try again?'

'What kind of a question is that?'

'I'm sorry, sir, but we need to acquire as much information as possible.'

Harry looked up at the blind's yellowing plastic slats and sighed. 'I don't know. The doctor says not.'

The constable put down his pen and stretched his fingers. 'Well, that's about it for questions. Unless you can think of anything else we should know . . .'

Harry shook his head and stood up. All this institutionalised sympathy was beginning to get on his nerves.

'We'll call you if we hear something, though to tell you the truth, the chances are slim.'

'I know.'

'Still, better safe than sorry. You've done all you could.' He paused. 'She's probably just taken herself off somewhere quiet for a rest.' The constable also stood. He seemed to be on the verge of offering to shake hands, the way a family doctor might after a particularly embarrassing man-to-man chat.

'Yes, probably,' said Harry, gritting his teeth.

'I don't care what you bloody well arranged. You're staying right where you are until I say you can go.'

Catherine stared at her fingers. One day she would allow herself to hit him: actually tighten her shaking hand into a fist and whack him as hard as she could between the eyes. Already he had driven her to punching her bedroom wall. The pain of slamming her taut knuckles into plaster and brick gave vent to an almost murderous frustration.

'And look at me when I'm talking to you,' he barked. He was standing so close to her she felt sick. He had been tinkering with the car since lunch, meticulously polishing the mirrors, the chrome. Checking the water. Checking the oil. He smelled greasy and sweaty. His breath was like sour milk and rotten cabbages. The tops of his fingernails were crammed black with accumulated muck. His sunburnt nose shone. His skin was pitted with little pools of oil. She passionately didn't want to look at him as he towered above her, swaying in self-righteous anger.

'I've got to phone Susan,' she said, refusing to be intimidated.

'Oh no you don't, young lady. I'll do that. You stay right

where you are. Here.' At random Ted grabbed one of Sheila's new books from the pile on top of the piano and flicked through. He had picked up enough about music by now to know that plenty of black notes squashed together meant difficult to play. 'Learn this,' he said, thrusting an open page in her face. Catherine blinked at him impassively. 'And if I were you I'd start right away. You'll do nothing else all weekend until it's perfect.'

You wouldn't know what perfect was, you thug, she thought, examining the page of manuscript with apparent calm. After a melodic start the treble line grew dark with semiquavers accompanied, below, by a sequence of chromatic chords. He had been trying this ever since the piano first arrived, four years ago; usually her mother intervened. She was out playing tennis this afternoon, a ladies four with friends from the club. A tournament or something.

'Not even Mummy can play this,' she muttered. The retreating figure paused in the doorway. Catherine held her breath.

'What was that?'

'Not even Mummy can play this,' she said again, too loud.

Slowly he turned to face her, pale with fury, steadying himself against the wall. 'Your mother's little finger is fifty times more talented than you will ever be, and don't you dare forget it.'

He locked the back door after him, pocketing the key, and stepped into the sunshine. It dazzled him. The garden was out of control, growing up faster than he could cut it back. Blossom shadows littered the grass. The roses seemed brighter than he remembered them last year, already their pink and yellow needed deadheading. The grass was an almost violent shade of green. He wheeled the lawn mower out of the garage. A thunderous G major, three octaves, two-hands, pounded from the open living-room window.

Kicking the engine to life, Ted pushed it to the bottom of the garden and the furious, invisible hands moved down a tone to F. The motor chugged, obliterating every last whisper of his stepdaughter's resentful performance and seducing him with a musical language of its own. A delicate whiff of petrol sputtered from one side of the engine, following him down. He liked the smell, it relaxed him. It reminded him of the war. So many engines. Tens of hundreds of blades of grass vanished hypnotically below the nose of the machine and his eyes glazed over, scanning for mines. He was hot, now, sweating as he reached the flowerbed. Across the fence he caught a glimpse of Mrs Thompson in her swimming costume, sun-bathing. He swivelled, ready for the uphill stripe, putting his shoulder to the bar. *Don't stop, you coward*, he told himself, ignoring the sweat as it slowly rolled from his forehead. When he was feeling energetic he could finish this job in under twenty minutes.

Watching from the spare bedroom upstairs, Catherine shook with excitement. The window was open already and the next lap would bring him directly into range. Her stomach cramped. She still couldn't believe she was going to do it. There would be hell to pay, of course, but it wasn't the thought of punishment that thrilled her so much as the realisation that what she was about to do would be considered 'going too far'. It would open a new dimension. It was as if she had discovered the atomic bomb. Was about to use it. She dared.

Again he turned to face the house, fifty feet away, and she ducked out of sight instinctively, her whole body trembling. Her palms were wet. She could have laughed with anticipation. The hum of the engine and the spitting sound of the blades grew steadily louder. She forced herself to count a slow twenty, and then peeked out. Fifteen feet. She heaved the bucket up onto the sill. Ten feet. Five feet.

The water fell in an elastic lump. Glittering for one, elongated second in the late afternoon sunlight. Slapping him across the head. Plastering his shirt to his back, his flannels to his legs. Drowning his shoes, the engine, the springy lawn. Catherine watched with horror as he turned around to look up at her, his face frozen in an expression of pure fear. The engine cut out. Not even birdsong interrupted the silence.

Sarah woke herself up, suddenly, as if from a nightmare. The nagging thought she hadn't quite been able to put her finger on all afternoon had just resurfaced as a question of life and death urgency. What would happen to the fish? They had been working so hard on the dam she had completely forgotten about it. George wanted to make a swimming pool, but what if the stream below ran dry?

She sat up in bed and waited for her pupils to expand. Slowly, the pale grey rectangle on her left turned into a window; the black oblong opposite became her wardrobe. Her sandals lay like small, sleeping cats in the middle of the floor. She climbed down and slipped them on, fumbling on the windowsill for her penknife. Outside, the corridor creaked as she tiptoed past Marion and Jamie's room and down the stairs, praying for Ollie not to bark. She could hear him moving about in the kitchen and lifted the latch quietly, pushing the door open. 'It's only me,' she whispered, reaching across the sideboard for the torch. 'Come on.' The spaniel padded after her silently, into the hall. Sarah unbolted the front door and shone the torch out into the yard.

It had stopped raining; pale clouds obstructed the moon;

grass, nettles and jasmine scented the still air. Cows shuffled in
the next-door field. Lured out under cover of darkness, hundreds of worms lay dew-bathing on the lawn. A fist-sized
toad hopped into the flickering yellow cone and sat there
blinking, astonished to find itself enclosed by light. Sarah ventured a few paces into the yard and tipped back her head,
turning slowly on the spot. The sky whirled. Never could she
remember having been surrounded by a night as dark and
alive as this. She wondered why she wasn't scared and
thought, immediately, of the story George had told about his
father's sheep disappearing one by one in mysterious circum-
stances. Adrenaline shivered up her spine. Suddenly the toad
leapt out of sight. There was the sound of rustling in the
grass. Then crunching.

'Ollie! Come on, boy,' she whispered loudly, torch-light
flickering up and down the gable wall as she patted her knees.
The dog advanced a few steps into the yard and then stopped.
No amount of persuasion would get him to move an inch further from the house. Sarah gave up and, keeping her attention
resolutely focused on avoiding the gleaming worms at her
feet, headed cautiously towards the stream.

At first it seemed to take forever, but gradually the earth
began to break up into dried-out hoof-prints. She was walking downhill. The clods grew softer, collapsing unexpectedly
beneath her weight. She could hear water. Falteringly, her
torch picked out the pool's jagged circumference. The mud
had settled; clear water lapped a few inches below the second
bamboo. Accompanied by the sound of splashing and gurgling, she crept downstream and shone her light into the trout
pool. Midges and fruit flies collected in the beam, whirling in

chaotic loops above the reflection. The largest, a thicker, darker dot, zig-zagged from side to side, dipping closer and closer to the surface. Once, then twice. A hair-line ripple flashed across the pool as the insect skimmed the shining meniscus and suddenly a black torpedo hurled itself into the torch-light. For an instant Sarah saw a silvery body curled and suspended in midair. Her heart thundered as the trout crashed back out of sight.

Ollie was still there when she got back to the house, standing exactly as she had left him, a few paces into the yard, legs planted square, leaning forward slightly as if he were about to strain at some invisible leash. He seemed to relax as she drew near, and led her noiselessly inside.

Mum's house is unbearably hot. The sun streams into her study through the open balcony windows and the radiators are still on. I can hear her moving about in my room, ironing probably, and trudge upstairs. It isn't used for much but ironing, nowadays; the bed stays made up and inessential books and clothes still wait on the shelves for a return to favour but the walls are spotted with abandoned nails, rectangles of minimalist, Blu-Tack art. I sit on my bed and look at our reflections in the mirror opposite. No one can believe we're mother and daughter.

'Did you get everything, then?' she sniffs, swishing the iron across what looks to me like a pillowcase but is in fact her white linen minidress.

'Yes, I'm just waiting for the butter to go soft. How can you iron in this heat?'

'It doesn't feel hot to me. Have you turned the oven on?'

'Not yet. God, it's hot.'

Ben calls people who tease the English for always going on about the weather philistines. He says they are obviously incapable of appreciating the infinite and subtle variations of light and atmospheric pressure which, together, constitute a typical

English day. He consciously tries to have at least one conversation about the weather every day. Mum, however, won't be
drawn. Instead we fall into a companionable silence, which
she finally breaks by asking, of the mirror as much as my
reflection in it, 'Do I really look that old?'

'You look great,' I reply.

'I look *old*.'

You *are* old, I want to say, what else did you expect? But I
know I will feel the same in thirty years. The eyelash at the
left-hand corner of my mouth won't brush away.

'I only recognise myself in the mirror downstairs, it's terrible.'

'When exactly is David coming?' I ask, to change the subject.

'Half past twelve. Will you still be here?'

'Of course I will.'

'Shall I invite him in? I'm sure he'd love to meet you again,
after all these years.' Her knees crick one by one as she reaches
down to unplug the iron.

'No, Mum. He isn't interested in me.'

'But I'd like to show you off.'

'I don't think so, Mum.'

'Are you sure?'

The butter is soft enough. It bulges between my fingers,
threatening to worm out through the folds in the greaseproof
paper like whipped cream or lemon icing. In the kitchen I
take the Gripstand and measure into it 10oz of dark brown
sugar. The butter is too weak to put up much resistance and
the sugar so luxuriously soft it slips from the sides of the bowl
like a liquid. They blend of their own accord.

Ben was originally impressed, and slightly dumbfounded, by this ritual. He thought it sweet of me to devote a day every year to baking, generous beyond the call of filial duty. Now, having eaten chocolate devil's food cake on a birthday of his own, he agrees it's a recipe well worth the effort, and when I explain that I regard it as a matter of fairness, a cake for a cake, like the paying off of an overdraft, he seems to understand. In fact it's more than that. I owe her more than twenty-one birthday cakes, but the debt will never be called in.

'It wasn't all his fault, you know.' Mum is in the bathroom, checking her roots.

'What?'

'When he left me.'

'I know.' I am sitting on the edge of the bath, watching her in the mirror.

'I haven't been sleeping with him.'

'Mum—'

'We just go out every now and then and get drunk together. Christ, we don't even reminisce!' She closes one eye and wipes the lid with a wad of cotton wool, removing yesterday's make-up. In the early years of their marriage, Dad made her a circular mirror surrounded by naked lightbulbs like the mirrors actresses in Hollywood musicals use. After David left, she scribbled 'Happiness is the Art of Never Looking Back' across the top in lipstick and nobody has ever got round to cleaning it off.

'Mum, I don't mind you going out with him!'

'I never said you did.'

'I just don't particularly want to meet him again – at least, not today.'

'Don't get angry.'

'I'm not angry, I'm ambivalent. I can't help worrying—'

'About what?' She chucks the cotton wool at the bin and misses, I lean forward helpfully to pick it up. Smudged with charcoal and creamy peach foundation, it smells of her. It resembles her in the way a relic resembles a saint.

'That you're going to end up hurt again.'

'Well don't. A lot has changed since then. I can look after myself. And he needs me . . .' Standing back, she examines her reflection, sucking her cheeks in to check the blusher, '. . . more than I need him. He's like a lonely old man. He says he wants to marry me.'

I find it hard to tell whether or not she is merely affecting nonchalance.

Thirty seconds more and the varnish would be dry. Catherine examined her fingernails in the mirror, admiring the thin exclamation marks of light which slithered to the tip of each smooth curve, disappearing as she tilted her spread hands. They were like shiny pink pearls. Or spades. Or teeth. She waved her skinny arms gracefully, in slow motion so as not to sweat, and prayed for the doorbell not to ring. Downstairs the reproduction antique grandfather clock chimed seven. She would have liked to imagine the house holding its breath for her, tense and silent with expectation. In fact it was always quiet like this. In summer you could hear the kitchen bluebottles from upstairs. Hot water seething into the radiators when the timer clicked on in winter. Dishwater vanishing down the plug. The flick of lightswitches blacking out room after room as her stepfather paced. A match, struck. Her mother sucking on a cigarette. Floorboards. Teaspoons. China.

Sheila sat in the kitchen opposite her husband, pen in hand, two towers of exercise books on the table before her, correcting misspelt comprehensions. Ted drummed his fingers on the Formica and stared at a photograph in *The Times*, letting its thousand black and white dots explode and collapse in and out of focus, waiting for some sign that she was aware of his presence, his existence. When she looked at him he would feel it. The hairs at the base of his neck would register the disapproval, like antennae. It was still light outside but the curtains were drawn. He had lost his bearings. When the doorbell went he raised himself, pushing up from the table like an old man. James Adams, suave and disconcertingly sincere, was invited to wait in the front room. A few seconds later, Catherine appeared at the top of the stairs, unsteady in her new high heels.

'Is he here?' she stage-whispered.

Ted stared up at her, not answering. 'Haven't seen that dress before,' he muttered at last.

'How do I look?'

'Come here.'

She floated down like a film star, one hand caressing the bannister.

'Closer.'

Stepping forward obediently, she straightened her shoulders, a soldier on parade, and lifted her head, careful not to meet his eyes. It was a pale blue chiffon evening dress, with tight-fitting, semi-translucent elbow-length sleeves and an extravagantly full skirt that brushed the knee. Her mother had found the pattern in Woolworths and Catherine had chosen the material. Ted hadn't been informed.

'Wait there.' He hurried upstairs. From the bathroom came the sounds of bottles toppling and she watched, bemused, as he hurried back, clutching a pink case.

'Dad?'

It was Sheila's make-up case. How many times had he watched her reach inside, a child at a lucky dip, for lipstick or mascara on her way out to work? 'Shut your eyes and do as you're told. You've smudged your eyeliner.' One hand held her upper arm as the other rummaged clumsily through the shiny, pink, foam-quilted compartments. 'Keep absolutely still, or I'll poke your eyes out.' Somehow it sounded more like a threat than a fatherly joke.

'Please, Dad, let me do it.' It was nice of him to have noticed but his hand was trembling, as usual, and what if James saw?

'Quiet,' he muttered, squinting at her eyelids. Something cool and wet flickered across her left eye and inched towards her temple. 'Now for the other one.' The brush clicked hollowly on the side of the pot as he squeezed its tip to a fine black point. 'That's better. Blusher next.'

'No.' She yanked her arm free and ran for the kitchen, pale blue chiffon puffing out behind as she went. Ted snatched a handful and pulled. The dress let out a sharp, inevitable gasp as Catherine flew forwards then stopped, too late, turning to face him with disbelief. 'My dress. MUM!'

'What is it?' asked Sheila from the kitchen, glancing up from her thirteenth exercise book.

'MUM!'

'It's all right, She, no need. I'm only teasing her.' He was fumbling through the bag again. 'Where's that lipstick your mother wears?'

The front-room door fell open a crack and James Adams peered through and coughed. Ted spun round.

'Get back in there,' he barked.

'Sorry, sir,' said James, slamming the door in his own face. Catherine watched with horror as he slid off the lipstick lid.

'Don't you dare,' she spat at him.

'Don't you dare,' he mimicked. 'Can't you take a joke?' He waved the naked lipstick closer and closer to her face until the soft red talon was so close she couldn't move without it smearing her.

'It's not funny,' she whispered, and stamped her foot, heel first, into his.

He heard his bones crack before he felt the pain. 'You little bitch,' he gasped, pushing her away from him. They stared at each other, furious, confused. Catherine, waiting for the inevitable reprisal, watched his face grow white. Finally he looked away. He sheathed the lipstick with steady hands and then, for a moment, seemed to hesitate. He turned from her at last, and shuffled upstairs.

'Cathy.' Sheila watched her daughter's raw, red eyes squeeze shut in the sudden electric light. 'I know you're not asleep.' She paused helplessly and, noticing the evening dress collapsed in a heap on the carpet next to the wardrobe, sighed. A shoe's toe poked out sideways from beneath the chiffon. 'Stop ignoring me, please.'

Catherine's eyes flashed open. '*You* can stop ignoring *me*!'

'And what in heaven's name is that supposed to mean?'

'You never stick up for me.'

She sighed again. She had hoped they would be allowed to forget the evening's earlier scene. 'What am I supposed to do?' she said.

'Tell him to leave me alone.'

'I can't.'

'Why not?' Catherine was leaning up on her elbows now, her scoured face pleading. Sheila perched on the edge of the bed.

'I just can't. When you have a husband maybe you'll understand.' For a moment she stared vacantly into the wallpaper, then snapped out of the reverie and said cheerily, 'Still, we've been through worse. You didn't much like James anyway, did you?'

'You know I did.'

'Oh.' She smoothed her skirt, picking off a ball of carpet fluff and pressing it, like a reminder, deep into the palm of her left hand. Then she stood up. 'I've left your bus money on the desk. Make sure you put it somewhere safe. Good night.'

Hunched, with his balding head between his knees, Ted sat on the bottom step and waited for his wife to come down. Hot, uncomfortable tears stickied the corners of his eyes, welled and dropped.

Sarah leaned against the windowsill. Outside, honeysuckle leaves quivered in the wind, tapping with delicate applause. Dapples of shadow and thick sunlight flickered across their palms. She waited five more rings to see if Marion or Jamie was in earshot, then picked up the phone. 'Hello?' Nobody answered but there was breathing at the other end of the line. 'Who's there?'

'Sarah?'

Tears immediately prickled the backs of her eyes and her heart seemed to gulp. 'Mum?'

'It's me. Your mother, remember?' Catherine was angry. Sarah's surging happiness soured. 'Who's with you?'

'No one. Marion and Jamie are in the garden.'

'Lucky them. Well, don't say I phoned.'

'Why?' Something clicked inside the receiver. 'Mum?' The dialling tone came on; she put the phone down. She felt sick to her stomach and her hands were shaking. Suddenly the telephone shrilled again and she leapt on it. 'Hello?'

'I can't believe you did that.'

'Mummy, did what?'

'Disobeyed me.'

'I won't any more. I promise. I won't tell them, Mummy, only please don't hang up again.' Two tears raced down her face in fits and starts.

'I will if you don't stop crying.'

'I'm not crying,' she sniffed. 'Where are you? Everyone's been so worried.'

'I'm all right. And you know I love you.' Catherine hesitated. 'I've got to go now.'

'Why?'

'Because I can't deal with this, that's why.'

'What do you mean?'

'I just can't. It's awful. I shouldn't have called.'

'I miss you. Will you phone again?'

'Maybe. Now put the phone down.'

'Mum, please.'

'Just say goodbye, will you, there's a good girl.'

'OK,' Sarah sniffed. 'I wish you were here.'

'I wish I was too, darling. But I'm not very good company at the moment. It's best for everyone if I stay away.'

'Not for me.'

'Yes, even for you. Now say goodbye and don't cry any more.'

'Goodbye.' As the phone went dead the kitchen door swung open. Sarah wiped her eyes and turned around. It was George.

'Hi there,' he said casually, strolling into the room.

Sarah wiped her nose on her sleeve and tried to smile.

'You've been crying.'

'No I haven't.'

He shrugged. 'Have you seen the dam?'

She shook her head miserably.
'It's broken.'
'Is it?' She sniffed. They went to look.

When Marion came in to turn the oven on ready for supper, twisting its button between the green rubbery fingers of her gardening gloves, she surveyed the kitchen, noticed the telephone off its hook, and tutted out loud.

'Sheila.'
'Yes?'

'I've got something to say.' Ted hesitated. 'I'm sorry.'

'What?'

'I'm leaving you.'

She looked up from her knitting sharply. 'What?'

That got her attention. He savoured the moment and went on. 'It's arranged. Perhaps I should have said sooner.'

At first she assumed he was just ragging them with another of his silly jokes. He would have been a good actor. Eleven pearl: remember, she told herself, jabbing the needles into the ball of wool. 'Say that again,' she bantered, 'only next time try not to laugh.'

'I didn't laugh. I wouldn't. It's no laughing matter.'

They had talked about it before, of course, several times. As a last resort. He had never been the same since coming back. Even she could tell that, and she had known him before only as one of the lads, the youngest, falling over himself to be friends with John. Now he was jumpy, scared, suspicious. But lots of men were. It didn't mean he actually had to leave them.

She looked at him. He was serious. 'Catherine, please go to your room.'

'No, let her stay.'

Catherine glanced at her mother for confirmation and closed her book. She folded her hands in her lap attentively, wreathed her fingers. All the colours in the room, the red chintz roses on the three-piece suite, the orange glow of the electric fires, her mother's navy blue sweater, seemed to shine, suddenly, with importance. She remembered it the way you remember a picture in a gallery. Corners of detail, here and there, jostling one above the other, into a vivid, hideous map of something else. Something completely different. The dialogue she remembers as if it were a scene from a play.

'You can't.'

'It's for the best. The doctor said.'

Her mother lit a cigarette. 'What does he know!'

Ted shrugged. 'He says I'm ill.'

'Nonsense, there's nothing the matter with you that a bit more holiday and a better job wouldn't cure.'

'Well, even if he's got it wrong, it's better than staying here.'

'Better for who?' she snorted.

'All of us.' He tried to smile at his stepdaughter. There was a silence. 'I can't take much more of this.' He reached for her hand and squeezed it mechanically. 'It may not be for long. But I want to go.'

'Well, I suppose we'll find some way of managing,' she muttered, shaking him off and picking the needles up again, withdrawing them inch by inch from the woollen heart. 'When do you leave?'

'Whenever I'm ready, the doctor says. I've got to hand in notice. A fortnight, perhaps.'

And that was it. No shouting, no tears. Her mother finished the row and went to lay breakfast. Her stepfather double-checked the windows a second time.

Mum leans forward over the sink, one eye open, one eye closed and trembling beneath the inky pad of her index finger. Yesterday's make-up is down the loo, the mascara on her eyelashes is fresh. The half-cup of coffee by the hot water tap is cold. Lying in a heap beneath the bidet are the white linen minidress she has decided not to wear, a grown-up looking, stone-coloured pencil skirt and a pair of jeans. David will be here any minute and she is still in her under-wear. I have been chivying her gently.

'Will you be here when I get back?' she says, streaking the second eyelash Tapenade.

I doubt it: the cake will only take thirty minutes; then there's another hour, at most, for the icing, washing-up . . . 'Why?'

She looks disappointed. 'Well, I've hardly seen you, have I? You've been in the kitchen all the time.'

'Do you want me to wait for you?'

'No,' she snaps the powder compact shut and drops it into her make-up basket, 'you'd better not. I'm meant to be work-ing, anyway. The first draft should have been in last week and I've had bloody Eleanor on the phone checking up on me too

many times already. No, you go on, get on with your life.
Make the most of it while you're still good-looking and
young.'

'Is that a compliment?'

She gives me her wryest smile. 'How will you get back?'
We are both careful not to use the word 'home' to describe
the flat where Ben and I have been living for the past two
months, albeit for different reasons.

'By bus.'

'Bus? Oh don't. I'll give you money for a taxi.'

'Mum, it's fine going by bus. It's practically door-to-door.'

'Maybe, but I can't bear to think of you travelling so slowly.'
She blinks at her face in the mirror. I'm back where I was
before, sitting on the edge of the bath with my feet on the
bidet. 'I may have many problems, but money isn't one of
them right now. I want you to take a cab and save yourself half
an hour of youth. Do it for me, make it my birthday present.
Where's my handbag?' I find her handbag in the study and leaf
through the compartments searching for the battered envelope
which traditionally holds her cash supply. There is an
umbrella, a pair of black leather gloves, a box of Panadol, an
emergency make-up purse which won't click shut, a Filofax
stuffed with American Express receipts, a rape alarm, keys.

'Have you found it?'

'Yes,' I'm still in the study, looking at the alarm.

'Well take out ten pounds, that should be enough.'

'Thanks.' She is curling her eyelashes when I return to the
bathroom, leaning over the sink and looking deep into the
mirror with her open eye. The doorbell rings. 'Shit! Let him
in, will you?'

'You do it—'

'What, like this?'

I am only too aware of her lacy underwired bra; like most women in this country I have more pairs of shoes. 'Just throw on the dress, it looked really good.'

'But now it's all crumpled . . . Go on, show him in downstairs and make conversation. Please!'

I am cornered, and though I know I'll probably have to meet him again sooner or later anyway, I suddenly, wilfully and absolutely don't want it to be today. I cannot recall having ever refused point-blank to do what she tells me; as I steel myself for it now the bell rings a second time.

'Go on, answer it,' she says, with a mixture of encouragement and desperation, 'or he'll think I'm standing him up and that will be the end of that.'

I think I will never forgive her for manipulating me like this.

Sarah thought of telling George about the trout but decided she would not. He was always going on about fishing, and she wasn't sure she could trust him not to kill it after she'd gone. She crouched on the bank and leaned closer, gazing through to the bottom of the water. The long, thin body of the fish emerged, an optical illusion, from the patterned sand and, for a moment, she forgot the telephone call, watching, utterly absorbed, as it danced on the spot, side-on to the current, rippling like a flag in the wind. She snapped a blade of grass and dropped it carefully onto the water. In a flash the trout disappeared. Marion's voice drifted down from the house, calling her in for supper. She ought to tell someone. They were worried, even though they pretended not to be. She knew because they jumped whenever the phone rang. From the way they broke off in mid-sentence, sometimes, when she came into the room, starting up again as soon as the door had closed behind her.

Darting out from its hole beneath the waterfall, the trout returned silently to the middle of the pool, bellying from side to side as if nothing had happened.

'Sarah! Supper!' Marion swished across the darkening lawn.

Blackbirds and thrushes flapped clear of her path. 'Where are
you?'

Sarah stood up. Together they turned back towards the
shadowy house, the sound of a telephone ringing through the
open kitchen window.

'Just another wrong number,' said Jamie as they came in.
He thrust his hands into a pair of oven gloves and opened the
grill.

Two days later she received a letter. 'Please don't show this letter to anyone else,' it began, and she took it outside to read
because she didn't want the others to see her cry. She took it
down to the trout pool, leaving a trail of footprints in the glittering morning dew which Marion held back from following.

The first time she read it through very quickly, to make
sure that it didn't say what she dreaded most of all. Then, as
the relief sank in, she read it a second time, trying to imagine
her mother come up to her bedroom at home to kiss her
goodnight, saying the words. She gazed at the handwriting
and her throat grew tight with love for the way the 'o's and 'a's
had twisted in with the other joined-up letters. Looking
closely she could just make out the pen-strokes, even though
it had only been written in Biro and, tilting it slightly, away
from the sun, the page seemed to fill with braille. She turned
it over and ran her fingertips across the paper, lightly, as if feeling her mother's face and hair. Finally, she read it a third time,
thinking now about the meaning of the words, something
inside her throat swelling again with pride. Of course she
forgave her, of course she understood.

When she had finished she folded it up and put it back

inside the envelope, taking care not to tear the sides any further. She wiped her eyes on the back of her hand and glanced
into the pool to check the trout was still there. Then she
walked back up to the house with the letter folded away
inside her sleeve. In her room she hid it beneath the lining of
her suitcase.

The door swung open, brushing easily across the mat to reveal a single letter, posted by hand, and a photocopied advertisement for home-delivered pizza. Harry stooped, as usual, to pick them up. As he straightened, a screwdriver whistled past his right ear and out into the front garden, clattering off the paving stones and through the open gate before finally coming to rest in the gutter.

'Watch out!' he yelled, stepping hastily out of range. Footsteps thundered across the ceiling directly above his head. 'Catherine? Is that you?'

'Fuck off.'

'You fuck off. You could have killed me. I'm coming upstairs.'

'Leave me alone,' she sobbed.

Running upstairs, he found her collapsed on the landing, crumpled against the wall, a bottle of Bacardi in one hand and a hammer in the other. Her handbag was looped around her neck and shoulder, resting in her lap like a small black animal. A suitcase blocked the entrance to the living room.

'Don't ever do that again,' he said quietly, the closeness of his escape still sinking in. 'You can play with your own life,

but not with mine. Got it?' He wanted to shake her, to wres-
tle the hammer from her grasp and land it neatly between her
eyes.

'Have you been following me?' she asked, not looking up.

'Shut up. Go to bed. You're drunk.'

Catherine unscrewed the bottle's lid and tilted its clear glass
neck to her lips defiantly, swallowing three times.

'I said go to bed.'

'Fuck off.'

'Get up!'

'Make me, you cunt,' she flashed back. Silently Harry raised
his fist. The veins on his forearm bulged with blood. For a
moment they stared at each other furiously, then she climbed
unsteadily to her feet and slid along the wall towards the bedroom door. It pushed open. 'Anyway, I can't,' she said, in a
different, suddenly childlike voice. 'There aren't any sheets.'

'Come on, just take your shoes off and lie down on the
blanket.' He had followed her in and watched, now, as she
undressed, the pieces of his heart shattering into smaller and
smaller shards as she fumbled hopelessly with the zip of her
black cotton skirt.

Downstairs Harry switched on the television, horse-racing,
and tried to read the newspaper, looking up whenever the
commentator drew breath. He had offered to stay until she
woke up – surprisingly it seemed to comfort her – but God
only knew when that would be, and meanwhile there was
nothing for him to do but sit there feeling uncomfortable,
bored, and claustrophobic. It was still officially his house, but
the place didn't feel like home any more. Come to think of it,
nowhere did.

Sunlight was streaming in through the conservatory windows and he focused on the muffled shouts of children playing outside, listening automatically for Sarah for a whole minute before he remembered where she was. He gave up on the paper and fiddled aimlessly with a piece of jigsaw – sky. Outside, the voices merged into an earnest chorus of *Dallas*. Marion and Jamie would start to wonder where he was. Would they be disappointed he couldn't come? He telephoned to tell them the news. He telephoned the police.

The coffee cup slid from rim to rim on its saucer, clicking cheerily. It was early evening now; he had watched the setting sun pink the walls of the houses opposite, the colours growing richer as they crept towards attics, loft-conversions and sealed up chimneys.

'Catherine, wake up.' He opened the curtains. Catherine heaved herself up onto her elbows.

'I don't want to be sober,' she muttered, squinting at the coffee, 'ever again.'

'Come on, drink up. We need to talk.'

'There's nothing to say.'

Harry bit his patience and returned to the bedside, putting the cup and saucer on her lap.

'Too hot.' She blew at the edge, spilling a few drops onto the naked duvet. 'Now look what you've made me do!' She rubbed the coffee deeper into the material and, for the first time, he noticed the scars on her wrists. They ran along the veins, a fierce crisscross of shiny pink lines, up the inside of each thin arm. 'Don't stare.'

'Sorry.' He sat down next to her, on the edge of the bed. The anger had left him curiously sympathetic, wistful almost. 'So. How are you feeling?'

'Numb. Drunk.' She blew at the coffee again but didn't sip. 'Totally alone. Betrayed. Abandoned. Cheated. Robbed. Vandalised. Shat on . . .' Perfectly calm, expressionless almost, her quiet voice seemed to evaporate in the brightness of the room.

'Is it getting better?'

She shook her head. 'It's not an illness, you know. It's a fact. I might never see him again. Fact. I could live for fifty more years and still never see him again. Fact. He might as well be dead.' She paused. '*I* might as bloody well be dead.'

'Don't say that.'

'Why not? It's how I feel.'

'Come on! There's more to life.' *Snap out of it,* he wanted to say.

'What more?'

'You know very well. You're a successful and respected writer, everyone at the paper seems to think you're brilliant, you live in a beautiful house, you have a lovely daughter . . .' he finished quietly, almost diffident. Platitudes had never worked with her. She wasn't even listening.

'I wish I was dead.'

'Why aren't you, then?'

'Because I didn't have enough pills to take.'

'Come on, Cathy, admit it,' he shook his head, 'you changed your mind. You took enough pills, the doctors told me so, but something made you change your mind.'

Catherine shrugged. 'Well, if it did,' she conceded, 'I wish

I could remember what it was, because there's nothing I can think of worth living for right now.'

Harry looked up from the carpet and saw that she was crying. He squeezed himself further onto the bed and put his arm round her shoulders, stroking her hair, combing it back from her face with his fingers. The tears seeped into her T-shirt. 'What can I do?' he asked, his voice full of tenderness.

'Nothing. There's nothing anyone can do.' She sniffed, wiping her nose, brushing her hand against his. Harry leaned across and kissed her lightly on the mouth.

'Salty,' he murmured, as if thinking out loud. Then, in a different voice, he said, 'I want to move back in, properly, and get Sarah home again.' He waited for her reaction. 'Let's try again.'

'No, it's no good. I've just got to sit this out.' It was as if she hadn't heard a word he'd spoken, he thought, deciding to leave the matter for a while. 'Pass my handbag, would you, I need a drink.'

'Me too.'

'Get your own,' she said, snatching it from him and spilling more coffee.

'You nearly killed me earlier this afternoon,' he reproached her mildly, recapturing the rum. 'I'd've thought the least you could do was offer me a drink.'

'I didn't know it was you.'

'Or you'd have thrown the hammer, I suppose.'

'Maybe,' she shrugged. 'Why did you come, anyway?'

'Just checking up on things. Where have you been all this time?'

'A hotel.'

'Where?'

'Does it matter?'

'Can you imagine how worried I've been?'

'Can you imagine how fucking alone I've been?'

He didn't answer. 'But you're staying here now.'

'Maybe. I haven't decided yet.' The bottle top spinned.

'Promise you won't disappear again without warning us—'

'Us? Who's "Us"?'

'Marion, Jamie, Sarah – everyone's been worried.'

'So you said.' Catherine shuffled deeper into the covers, she had been awake for long enough. 'It wouldn't help, you know.'

'What wouldn't?'

She closed her eyes, drowsily. 'You moving back in.'

'It might.'

'It wouldn't.'

'It might.' He brushed a lock of hair from her forehead and watched as she slowly fell into a breathless, restless sleep.

Rain. Falling monotonously hour after hour over the Vale of York and the Howardian Hills, over Scarborough, drenching holiday-makers, turning the beaches into shiny strands of orange mud, diluting rock-pools, pricking the surface of the sea with their ceaseless hiss, like radio interference. Cloud-bank after cloud-bank, an armada of rain, anchored over north-east England for the whole of the foreseeable future, run aground on the hills above Kirkbymoorside, scraping the tops of the conifers and giant spruce in the forestry plantations east of Hovingham, dulling the golden statuary on the roof of Castle Howard with its noisy downpour.

Torrents of rain cascaded over the roof tiles like a river in spate, splashing and twisting all the way down in a shallow, never-ending waterfall, gushing into the drain. Overspills dribbled intermittently from the eaves in long, slow silvery lines, sputtering onto the sodden dog-daisies below. A continuous barrage of water-pellets peppered the leaves of the lilac tree while from the orchard rose a mysterious hush: droplets slithering from leaf to leaf to leaf and falling at last near silently to earth. It was as if the whole farm were one giant musical instrument, ticking and whispering to the skies.

The branches of the broad leaves drooped above their jet black, saturated trunks, glittering dimly in the cheerless pewter light. Wheat and barley heads clung heavily to their stems and prayed for no wind.

Marion loved rain. It was her weather. Its enclosing quietness put her at ease. She loved that it was necessary and inconvenient and therefore complicated. She loved its liberating claustrophobia; in the field looking up from her boots to see a sodden countryside utterly abandoned, utterly hers. She loved the washed-out colours of wet things, their sudden intensity and their soft, unassuming shines. She loved their sounds.

She threw a stick for the dog and he tore off, bounding across the rough meadow, weaving in and out of thistle clumps, water flying from his paws like dust. There was not another human being in sight. A blackbird, more densely black than she had ever seen one look before, darted out from the hedge. Ollie galloped back and dropped the stick at her feet. She patted him, affectionately scrunching the warm, soggy fur of his neck. He licked her hand. She was twenty-four days late. She could almost weep. The thought of it nudged her delicately inside, like swallowed air.

'We could mend it.' Sarah tugged absentmindedly at a loose straw, pulling it free. She held it up to her eye and squinted down the hollow stalk, the garden shrinking to a tiny, pale green dot. They had set up camp in the Dutch barn behind the house. George had bagsed the swing. Outside, long straight silvery spears enveloped the trees and fields with a kind of vertical, slicing mist. The lawns and rosebushes seemed to steam.

'What's the point?' he said, leaning back as he flew towards the nettle patch. 'They'll only kick it down again. Stupid bloody cows.'

'We could put up a fence.'

'Then they'll have nothing to drink.'

'Ask your dad to move them to another field.'

'Don't be an idiot.'

'You're the idiot.' She blew through the straw, which whistled feebly, then sucked in. Fresh air blasted the back of her mouth. She coughed. George swung higher. She coughed again. 'Yuk, I've swallowed a fly!'

'Perhaps you'll die.' The swing's frame creaked accompaniment. George had manoeuvred himself into a crouching position and now he stood up, straightening his knees cautiously and inching his hands one by one to the top of the chains. Rain clattered against the corrugated-iron roof like stones. He looked down at the ground rushing backwards and forwards, closer and further away, beneath his feet. 'Flies don't have digestive systems, you know. They puke on their food and digest it outside their bodies and then eat it.'

Sarah removed her finger from her throat, choking. 'No they don't.'

'They do, I promise.'

'Liar.'

'I promise. Ask anyone.'

Sarah approached the swing. 'Come on, it's my go now.'

'I'll push you.'

'OK.' She lifted her feet from the ground and felt herself go heavy as George's hands pressed into the middle of her back.

'You weigh a ton.'

'I do not.'

He let go, jumping out of the way as she swung back unevenly, the chains twisting. 'Sarah,' he said, deciding to ask, 'what happened to your cousin?' His hands were at her back again, his fingertips pressing in just below her shoulderblades.

'What cousin?'

'Mum says you had a cousin who died.'

'Toby.'

'Toby.' He said it carefully, as if the names of dead people were somehow difficult to pronounce, and waited for her to continue. The rain on the roof sounded very loud. 'Did he really get run over?' The swing flew higher and higher; its rusty frame creaking. 'Did he?'

'Yes.' Sarah focused on the nettle patch and tried not to think about how queasy she was feeling.

'What was it like?'

'I don't know, I wasn't there.'

'But what happened?'

'He was killed. Stop pushing, will you.'

'Scaredy!' He pushed her again, as hard as he could. The nettles seemed to leer at her. 'Don't, I feel sick!'

'Tell me what happened to Toby.'

'It's none of your business.'

'So?' His hands bit into her.

'Marion doesn't like people talking about it.'

'Why? Was it her fault?'

'Don't be stupid. She just doesn't like to be reminded.'

George walked away. He leaned against a post with his back to Sarah, half-exposed to the weather, staring out at the top lawn and the vegetable patch. Huge, shell-like rhubarb leaves twitched in the rain. Marion walked into view. She had taken off her hat and her wet hair curled at the ends. She seemed to float across the grass like a ghost. Goosebumps shivered up George's spine. Ollie followed her into the house.

Slowly, Sarah swung to a stop. 'Want another go?'

He shrugged.

'Let's go into the granary, then.'

'Why?'

'I'll show you something, but you've got to promise you won't tell anyone.'

Marion kicked off her boots and rushed to the kitchen, her damp socks marking footprints on the tiles. Ollie trailed behind. The answer-machine clicked in. A woman's voice, gently Scottish, spoke after the tone. 'Mrs Heath—'

She pounced on the receiver. 'Hello?'

'Mrs Heath?'

'Yes?'

'It's Joyce Keay here – from St Margaret's.'

'Matron,' she knew she had recognised the voice. 'Hello, is everything all right?'

'I'm afraid not . . .'

Marion leaned against the windowsill and stared at the phone, letting the words dissolve into a meaningless blur of high and low. Front and back vowels, dotted with ticks and lisps and pauses.

'We're not meant to be here, remember. If you tell anyone, I'll kill you.' She drew the bolt and pushed the door ajar. George slipped in sideways. 'Budge up.'

'There isn't much room,' he whispered

'I know.'

'What's this?'

'Furniture, stupid.' Their eyes adjusted to the gloom.

'Look!' said George, pointing at the tangle of legs and surfaces. A long refectory table emerged, crouching above a low oak trunk. A dismembered writing desk balanced on top of it. Three wardrobes and a glass-fronted cabinet stood in a row to the left, the severity of their blank veneers compromised by the upside-down backs of a set of dining-room chairs. 'They look like they've got antlers.' Carved legs tickled the rafters. Daylight dribbled in through the obstructed windows. A row of bedsteads, upended and reminding George of some toothless, monster jaw continued the defences to the right. A carefully placed folding card-table filled the gap by the furthest wall.

'Follow me,' said Sarah, lifting up the leaf and ducking into the hole below. They crept through into a narrow passage. After five steps the furniture bank gave way, suddenly, to a corner of open space. A rug had been rolled out and an armchair dragged free of the heap. Fat black bin-liners littered the floor like giant lumps of mould. George grinned silently with amazement.

Untying the knot at the top of the nearest bag, Sarah rummaged around inside, as if it were a lucky dip. She lifted out a small, blue T-shirt.

'What's that?'

'It was Toby's.' She draped it carefully over the arm of the chair and dipped her hand inside again.

'Hey, I had pyjamas like that,' said George, 'only mine were red. They came from Marks and Spencer.'

Sarah looked inside the neck. 'Label's been cut out.' She held it up against George. 'Too small.'

He fidgeted uncomfortably. 'Are you sure we should be doing this?'

'I thought you wanted to know about Toby.'

'Yes,' he answered doubtfully. Sarah had already moved on to the next black bag.

'This one's got all his old toys in.'

'Let's see!'

Marion put the phone down and tried to remember what the day had been like before it rang. She had wet hair. It was lunchtime. She had been about to cook something. Any second now Sarah, and George too probably – the two of them seemed to be inseparable nowadays – would wander in wanting food. She opened the fridge and took out a box of eggs, but the thought of breaking them made her stomach turn. She put them in a saucepan with water and switched the ring on. Sarah would have to be told, of course. And Harry. Small bubbles began to form on the bottom of the pan.

The toy bag was empty; it lay scrunched up on the armchair, hidden beneath a layer of baby clothes. George and Sarah sat like islands in a Lego and Airfix sea. The cuddly toys of Toby's infancy had been chucked, without ceremony, into a heap in the corner. His board games towered precariously by the wall.

George was counting Dinky cars, lining them up in motorway formation, bumper to bumper, muttering running commentary under his breath. 'What car was it?' he asked suddenly, out loud.

Sarah looked up from her Rubik's cube. 'Was what?'

'You know . . .' Silently he pushed a tin-coloured Mercedes into the nearest Lego man.

Sarah shrugged. 'The driver didn't even go to prison.'

The Mercedes reversed with a shriek, severing the Lego man's head from his body. Slowly, separately, they ascended to heaven, jerking as if on a string. Sarah giggled. A gust of wind blew rain against the window, making them look round. George slipped the Dinky car into his pocket.

One of the eggs had cracked. The white escaped in poly-styrene clouds and thick scum foamed at the edges of the pan. Marion's forehead glistened with steam. She wiped the oven clock, wondering not for the first time in her life how long it takes a body to go cold. She had been with Toby when he died, in the hospital, stroking his sticky hair. The doctors had made her leave almost as soon as it was over, which she regretted every day. The clock's face misted up again. They must be done by now, she thought, leaving them in anyway. For God's sake, where was Sarah?

She put her cold, damp boots back on and wandered out to the barn. The swing hung motionless and dry beneath its rusting corrugated-iron roof; there were footprints in the soft, dusty earth around its frame, which disappeared into the muddy grass.

'Sarah! Lunch! Where are you?'

George and Sarah froze. 'Quick! Where's the bag?' She started to shovel the Lego into a heap in the middle of the carpet. George looked ruefully at his motorway and then, with a terrible sweep of his hand, brushed it into a single, cataclysmic pile-up. He stood up to find the bag. Outside, Marion thought she heard something, but nothing but chair legs and mahogany veneer could be seen through the window. She listened harder, trying her best to ignore the rain's incessant patter. A floorboard creaked.

Slowly, incredulously, she walked up the mossy steps and pushed the door ajar. The granary filled with the sound of held breath. Marion ducked below the flap at the end of the card-table. She crept along the secret corridor and stared.

The children had stopped what they were doing and were crouched, one on each side of a half-empty bin-liner, their hands full of toys. More toys lay scattered across the carpet. In the corner, a small, upside-down, no-longer-white rabbit balanced on its pink cotton nose. Nobody breathed.

'I think you should go home now,' she said at last to George, who had been staring studiously at the floor. 'Sarah, come and find me when you've finished tidying up in here. There's something I need to tell you. I'll be in the kitchen.'

Harry phoned Catherine to test the water. Marion had promised she still didn't know and insisted that it would be best if he told her face to face, so all he said was that he would be coming round later and could she please not throw anything at him this time. She promised to try.

It was dark when he arrived. He went through the house from room to room switching on lights, and crept last into the bedroom. Catherine lay in bed, fully dressed, with the covers thrown back. Her brushed hair shone, spread out on the pillow behind, like a pale, wavy halo. Her eyes were black with kohl. Her glossy lips thinned with disapproval as he came in.

'You're late,' she muttered, staring pointedly at the ceiling. 'I had to cancel the reservation.'

'What?'

'Dinner. I thought you were going to take me out.'

'I never said that,' he answered, leaning awkwardly against the frame of the door. She kicked off her high heels and he suddenly noticed the dress she was wearing: red silk, with little cupped sleeves and a low-cut neckline.

She watched him noticing. 'New this afternoon. I bought

it to cheer myself up. Never mind, one more disappointment can't do me any harm.'

'Just as well.'

'Why?'

'Nothing.' He inched closer to the bed and sat down next to her, somewhat reluctantly, on the edge. 'Catherine, I don't know how to tell you this. Your mother died this morning. The hospital tried to phone but you were out, so they rang Marion. It was a peaceful ending, they said, whatever that means.' He felt for her hand and squeezed it. Catherine smiled emptily.

'Well,' she said at last, blinking hard. 'Now I really am.'

'What?'

'Completely and utterly alone.' She thrust her free hand under the pillow, fumbling for the bottle. Bacardi sloshed inside its glass.

'Come on, Cathy. Don't do that. I know how bad it feels but please, don't get drunk.'

'Stay drunk, you mean.'

'Whatever. Come on,' he snatched at the opened bottle, splashing white rum over the dress and the duvet. As she lunged after it he caught her by the arm, dropping the bottle, and pushed her back against the pillows. Bacardi seeped into the dark blue carpet, filling the room with alcohol fumes.

'You can have no idea,' she said, gazing sadly into the stain, 'how difficult it is going to be for me to get that out.' She closed her eyes as if to indicate that as far as she was concerned the conversation was at an end. Her body went limp in his arms but Harry would not relax his grip. He stared into her face. Tiny specks of light glittered in the kohl-like stars and her eyes circled slowly beneath the lids, exploring an orange darkness. She could feel his look. For a moment she even enjoyed it.

'Kiss me,' she said. 'I've run out of tears.'

D avid looks taken aback when I let him in. The possibility that, after all these years, he might have come to the wrong address flickers across his brown, wrinkled face, followed by recognition. We say hello simultaneously and there is an awkward pause as he wonders whether to shake hands.

'Mum's not ready yet,' I offer, in my friendliest voice. 'She'll be down in a minute.'

'Right. I'm probably early anyway.' He pushes his hands deep into the pockets of his jeans (he still wears jeans) and looks at me sideways.

'So,' I begin. 'How are you?'

'Fine. And you?'

'Yes, fine.'

'So grown up.'

'I suppose so. People say I look about fifteen.' I am examining my half-bitten nails.

'And you're a journalist.'

'Trying to be. Like Mother . . . She thinks I'm making a terrible mistake. I think she wishes I'd gone to work in the City!'

'She's proud of you.'

'I'm proud of her.'

'Of course,' he pauses. 'And how's your father? Still work-ing in the same old place?'

'Where else?' Some people work to live. He lives for work: it is the backdrop to all my lasting images of him. 'He says he wants to sell up and move to the country and make a garden. Some hope!'

'Good old Harry! You must give me his number. I'd like to see him again, catch up.'

'Yes.' For a long moment there is nothing I can think of to say. 'I'm sorry Mum's taking so long. Would you like to sit down? Come in.'

'Thanks.' As he follows me into the drawing room, the bur-glar alarm goes off. We jump. Rushing back to reach the cupboard before the police are notified and Mum receives a massive fine for wasting their time, I crash into him and we stag-ger towards the grand piano like inebriated ballroom dancers.

'God, I'm so sorry.' Disentangling myself, I punch in the code – the date of Mum and Dad's wedding – and wait for the screeching to cease. David leans against the piano, grey-faced and trembling with shock. When I was little he used to hook his hands through my armpits and whirl me round and round; it was called aeroplanes, and sometimes he would do it hold-ing one of my wrists and one of my ankles instead. Now he seems terribly fragile. I picture him shuffling down the slimy steps by his front door, more slippery now than I've remem-bered them, fumbling in his pocket for the key. I don't know why, but suddenly I am overwhelmed with pity.

Halfway through my third apology, Mum bursts in. 'Is everything OK?' She is wearing the minidress, creases and all.

'Cathy, we've got to talk.' Harry was staring up at the ceiling, he didn't want to catch her eye.

'What about?'

'Your mum. You – we, need to think about the funeral. You'll have to come to Yorkshire for a while, sort things out.' He threw back the duvet.

'Don't do that. I'm cold.'

'Put some clothes on then. I'm hot.'

Goosebumps prickled her breasts. 'You've got a bloody nerve. It's my bed, you know.'

So this was the reconciliation. Harry rolled away from her and groaned. It had been a nostalgic performance and he was regretting it already. They could never be friends; even in this state she got too much pleasure from the fight. He sat up stiffly. He felt old.

'Where are you going?'

'Home, I suppose.'

'The office?'

He nodded, refusing to look at her flushed, astonished face.

'But what about me? You can't go now. My mother's just died.'

'Fat lot you seem to care about it,' he said, buttoning his shirt.

'And we've got to talk,' she went on, panic distorting her voice, 'about funerals, you said.'

'It'll have to be another day.' He shuffled into his slip-ons and smoothed his hair. His hands were trembling.

'Please don't go, Harry. Please! I don't understand. What happened?'

'I made a mistake. I'm sorry. I've got to go.' He hesitated, dizzy with the thought of trying to translate his feelings into a decent explanation. Then he shrugged and walked out.

Outside it was still warm. The cherry trees loomed like dense black shadows above the pavement and the sky was a soft pinky brown. Litter waited in the gutter for a stroke of wind. Standing alone in empty pools of light the lampposts held their breath. Harry unlocked the boot of the Rover, fumbling for his wrench; his whole body fizzed from the fingertips in. He stepped back from the car for a moment, and gripped the handle tight.

Glass shattered. Chips of paint exploded into coloured daggers and ugly dents thundered against the sunroof. As he struck the metal work again and again, the noise built up into a crescendo of howls. Slowly the fizzing stopped and his veins went quiet. The Rover hummed. At last he relaxed his grip. He rolled down his sleeves and brushed the glass from the driving seat, got in. Drove home.

'Marion?'

'Catherine? Do you know what time it is?'

'Well it's not as if either of us is getting up for work in the morning, so what does it matter what the fucking time is!'

'What is it? What's wrong?'

'I want you to organise the funeral.'

'I hadn't—'

'You always were her favourite and, seeing as you're local and you've done it before – I'll pay of course.' There was a stunned pause on the other end of the line. 'Well?'

'I'm not going to talk about this right now. Phone back in the morning,' said Marion, hanging up.

Catherine rang back. 'I want to speak to my daughter.'

'She's asleep.'

'Wake her.'

'No.' She hung up again, this time leaving the receiver off the hook.

Sarah listened for Marion's return, the squeak shut of the door downstairs, the creaking passageway. She wanted to say sorry but, every time she began, Marion would change the subject, or look away, or simply turn her back and walk off. She thought about her gran not being alive any more and tried to feel sad.

Jamie glanced across the table from Marion to Sarah and back again, trying to decide which of them looked worse. His wife's face was grey from lack of sleep, and dark shadows underlined each puffy eye. Her hair had turned frizzy in the previous day's rain, yet somehow contrived to look simultaneously lank. She sipped her tea as if it were medicine. All through breakfast Sarah had not smiled once. She too seemed tired. Her eyes were glazed and lifeless, her expression set. Neither of them had touched their food. Jamie didn't like to think himself a cynic, but he suspected this had little or nothing to do with yesterday's bad news. He considered making one last attempt at conversation, then shuffled back his chair and stood up, abandoning the idea. He carried his plate to the sideboard and silently returned for the jam jars, the milk and the butter. He checked his watch; turning up early for once wouldn't do any harm, he supposed. 'I can hardly bring myself to leave you both,' he announced fondly, 'but I must.' He gave Marion a chaste little kiss on the forehead. 'Phone if you need me.'

She nodded.

'Bye then.'

'Bye,' they murmured. The kitchen door banged shut and Jamie's office shoes slapped across the tiles in the hall. Ollie barked. The car revved modestly. Marion got up to clear away the rest of breakfast.

'I'll do that if you like.'

'No thanks, pet. I've got a lot of things to do today. I'll get through them quicker without your help.'

Sarah stared glumly at the cold toast on the side of her plate. She was starving.

'Have you finished, love?' Marion picked up the plate and dropped its contents into the bin. 'I've got some phone calls to make now; it's a lovely day, why don't you go outside?'

She wandered out barefoot into the sharp sunlight. It was already warm and the puddles had almost all evaporated. The track was dry. A huge black bee flew past, nearly deafening her and she trailed after it aimlessly, round the front of the house as far as the buddleia. Dozens of red admirals, peacocks and tortoiseshells flapped without apparent care from bough to bough, unfurling their needle-tongues deep into the centres of its tiny purple flowers. One of the peacocks had settled on the wall instead and hung there, its wings splayed, sunning. Close-up she could see the individual strands of its dusty fur, glittering in the light like powder. The patterns disappeared.

Marion shook the dishwater from her hands and opened the Yellow Pages, flicking backwards to F for funeral parlour. One entry leapt out at her in bold: E.P. Kendal & Sons, 219 Wilton Road, York. She could still remember the number off by heart. She covered it with her index finger and scanned the list for an Oswold telephone code.

The car door slammed. Sarah stopped pulling blades of grass from the dry-stone wall and watched as the Citroën rolled slowly down the track towards her, Ollie following at a distance. The window wound down and Marion leaned across the passenger seat. 'I'm going to Oswold.'

'Can I come?'

'Best not, pet. I might not be back by lunch, so just make yourself a sandwich. Promise me not to turn the cooker on.'

'OK.'

'You'll be all right.'

Sarah nodded. The Citroën vanished between the trees.

She went to investigate what was left of the dam. The pool had returned to its exact, irregular oval and the water was clear. The mud and twigs and leaves they had used to stuff the cracks had been washed away long ago. A heap of stones, half-submerged and only approximately wall-shaped, was all that remained. The bamboo measuring sticks had disappeared into the mud. The culprits had left behind a fossilised stampede of deep, sucking hoofprints, but were nowhere to be seen. Sarah waded in, shivering as the black slime oozed against the arch of her foot and between her toes. Slowly, her icy feet went numb.

She looked up from her silvery reflection, suddenly aware of the lazy drone of an engine in the distance. Wading through the pool, she followed the sound up into the meadow. The air smelled sweet. Bit by bit the pea-field bobbed into sight. The engine grew louder. A tractor lurched out from the shadow of the hedge, trailing a wide, complicated-looking metal contraption after it. George followed at a distance, scything the demolished peas with a long, straight stick which whistled as he whipped it through the air. *He never told me they were harvesting today*, she thought, fingering the penknife in her trouser pocket. She waved, calling out to him, but her cry was eaten up by the chattering of smashed stalks and he didn't look round. *I'll kill myself, and then he'll be sorry*, she thought, turning back reluctantly to face the farm. Fluffy white clouds spilled up from the horizon. Dried mud peeled from her feet in cakes.

So now they've gone and the house is quiet again and thick with baking. It smells of rainy Saturday afternoons and staying up late to watch Humphrey Bogart films; it smells of wrapping paper and chocolate. Childhood is only being allowed to have what other people give you, so there never was anything I could do about Mum. No one suggested it would help, but I tidied my room and finished my homework anyway, hoping, the same way I'm hoping now, that little things might make a difference: lilies, cake. Sometimes I can get her to laugh at my jokes.

Unlocking the conservatory doors I step out into the heat; a slice of shadow inches out from the brick wall as the sun slips down behind the roof. As you grow away from them, the houses and gardens of your childhood are supposed to shrink into pale realities of their fantastic, mysterious former selves. But somehow the garden square, with its bleached, dusty grass and moth-eaten privet hedges, anonymous shrubbery, secret bush-tunnels, hideaways and other sites appropriate for the burial of small, unfortunate birds, seems just the same. I roll up my sleeves and close my eyes. Desultory builders tinker with the scaffolding on the pistachio-coloured house opposite, knocking its bolted braces loose and shouting to one another as the poles slide free. A nanny sunbathes in the middle of the lawn, where Joshua used to stand.

The cake is cooked, its three thin layers tipped out, unbroken, onto the cooling racks, an even, chocolatey brown. Mum has come back early from lunch. As sugar, golden syrup, butter and cooking chocolate slide together in the pan, she stands by the window, looking up into the branches of the cherry tree.

'What happened?' I ask, for the fourth or fifth time, still unable to decide if the expression on her face is one of triumph or defeat.

'I'm not exactly sure,' she says at last, 'but I think I've blown it.'

I stir the thick, rich mixture slowly round the bottom of the pan and glance at the sugar thermometer.

'He asked me. Instead of going on, as usual, about how nice it would be if, one day, we decided to live together and if we were going to do that then maybe we should just bow to convention and get married. Have a party. Instead of that he actually popped the bloody question. Straight out. Just like that. Before the waitress even had time to take our order.' She speaks in the distant voice of one in shock. 'I thought I was going to pass out. I had this sudden rush of adrenaline.'

'And?'

'And then, when I said no, he went all sad-looking and quiet.'

'You turned him down?'

'Of course.'

'I thought that you wanted to get married.'

More than anything else in the whole wide world. David was the only one who could ever make me happy.

Can't I make you happy, Mum?

Oh, Sarah, it's not the same . . .

'Don't be silly, Sarah. What on earth would I want to get married for? You're the one who wants to live happily ever after, not me.'

'But you told me you loved him.'

'That was more than ten years ago!'

But you told me he was your kindred spirit, I say to her in my imagination. *You were going to love him for as long as you lived and into eternity, and take him back whenever he came, whatever he had done. I've got the letter. It says so. That's why I didn't mind . . .* The mercury nudges up inside its glass and the fudge icing mixture bubbles steadily. 'Was he upset?'

When she was still a very young child, the story goes, someone asked my mother what she'd choose if she was given three wishes. A rocking-horse, she said, a four-poster bed, three more wishes. She shrugs. 'A bit. He must have known I'd turn him down, though, otherwise the bastard would never have asked. What do you care, anyway? An hour or so ago you couldn't even bear to meet him.' She pauses, ostensibly to examine the cakes. Then she says, in a quiet voice, 'I can't have hurt him nearly as much as he hurt me.' In an instant I am convinced that this is what she's been aiming at all along.

'And no, it's not about revenge,' she finishes, not quite reading my mind.

I want to cry. I stir more vigorously. She picks her handbag up off the floor and threads it over her shoulder.

'Jesus Christ, Sarah! Where are your loyalties? After all he did to me,' she says, stalking from the kitchen. She takes the phone off the hook and climbs into bed.

'Are we nearly there?' Sarah nudged her father and repeated the question. The adults smiled wanly. Marion stroked her empty, black leather gloves, smoothing them against her knee, and looked through the window at the outskirts of the town inching, inching by. On the pavement a group of boys glanced up from their chip bags to point at the hearse. A blue cortina pulled out into the right-hand lane to overtake. She held her breath.

'Can we have the window open? I'm baking.' Sarah shuffled awkwardly on the sticky seat. 'I hate this dress!'

Harry pressed a button in the door and the window slid down; petrol fumes invaded the limousine. A light breeze blew stray hairs into Marion's face. Jamie sweated quietly in the opposite corner, nervously mouthing the address. Low-built red-brick terraces gave way to a playing field bounded at the far end by a black iron railing. The limousine swung left into a smooth, straight, tarmacked drive lined with poplars. Out of sight, a lawn mower muttered between the headstones.

There was a small glass building squatting pretentiously at the far end of the avenue, flanked by parking bays and

identified as the chapel by the thin brass cross hanging to
the left of the door and the slow stream of mourners shaking hands outside. The vicar stood in his doorway,
consoling the emergent bereaved with appropriately cheer-
ing or respectful platitudes. Car doors slammed and rear
lights flickered on and off in the sunshine as friends and
family manoeuvred in the forecourt. Sarah looked puzzled.

'You said hardly anyone would come.'

'How strange,' Harry frowned. 'That must be the funeral
before.'

'Oh,' she said, relieved that no one, as promised, would see
her in Marion's old dress.

Their convoy pulled into the verge and stopped, allowing
the queue of oncoming cars to pass. At the sight of another
coffin, some of the mourners looked away. Jamie folded the
address and slipped it into his pocket, catching Marion's eye.
He could see what she was thinking and he wanted to put his
arms round her, holding her tight as he had held her on the
way to Toby's funeral. He tried to smile instead. Marion
watched his face contort. The last car disappeared and they set
off once more, gliding the final few metres at walking pace.
Six men in cheap black suits strolled into view from behind
the chapel, dropping their cigarette butts on the tarmac and
adopting a collectively serious expression as they approached
the hearse. The vicar hurried towards them.

'Mrs Heath?' he questioned, guiding Marion through the
limousine door with a wave of his hand. 'So pleased to meet
you at last, but on such a sad day for the family, alas.' They
shook hands. 'I do apologise for the overlap – the chapel was
quite full and then the service, unfortunately, over-ran. If you

don't mind waiting five more minutes . . . we're not quite
ready yet – I need to reset the hymn numbers et cetera. This
is most unusual. I really am very sorry.' He smiled disarmingly.
'You are all welcome, of course, to come inside to wait, say a
few private prayers of your own perhaps. Mrs Ellis is here
already.' He turned to go. 'Ah, there she is now.'

Marion stared incredulously as her cousin wandered out
from the shadow of the chapel, squinting into the sunlight,
fluffing her back-combed bob and rearranging the long, black
chiffon scarf which floated dreamily about her shoulders, trailing almost to the ground. She removed a pair of sunglasses
from her handbag and put them on, walking unsteadily
towards the hearse. Ignoring Marion, she peered in through
the window, cupping her eyes to the glass. The coffin was pale
and silver trimmed; a single bouquet rested on top. A sudden
joyful shriek broke the silence.

'Mum!' The woman in black turned sharply and removed
her sunglasses. Sarah ran towards her, then stopped short.
They looked at each other, neither knowing quite what to do
or say next. In the background, Marion leaned heavily against
the limousine.

'Hello,' Sarah said at last, with strange formality. 'How are
you?'

'Drunk, how are you?'

She shrugged. 'Dad's here,' she added rather obviously, as
Harry hurried round the back of the car to speak to Marion.
Jamie strolled up, wiping his hands.

'Catherine, love,' he said warmly, peering into her dulled
brown eyes. He kissed her, once on each cheek. 'We're so
pleased you decided to come. It's good to see you. I'm sorry

about your mother. Shall we go in? It may be cooler.' His hand pressed lightly on Catherine's back as he guided them towards the beaming vicar.

'Are you all right?' Harry looked anxiously into Marion's pinched face.

She gave a thin smile. 'Surprised. Can we wait out here for a moment?'

'Of course.' He paused. 'I'm sorry,' he said at last, 'about all this. My family seems to be taking over your entire summer.'

'It's my family too.' She paused, nodding towards the chapel as Catherine disappeared inside. 'We used to be so close, you know. Like sisters. I don't know, I suppose we still are, really. Deep down.'

He nodded. 'I had hoped that doing the funeral might have helped – distracted her. Like throwing a dog two sticks.' He shrugged, glancing at the hearse. 'We all knew Sheila didn't have long – I was stupid enough to be pleased, you know, that it had happened now . . . I'm sorry you've had to do it. Things can't have been easy.'

Marion patted his arm. Far away an ambulance turned into the avenue. The tarmac seemed to ripple in the heat. She gazed at the shimmering poplars and up at the seam of blue that ran between them like a sky canal. Twenty-nine days, she thought, staring into the cornflower. It was her secret, enough to get her through any family disaster. The ambulance grew larger and larger but didn't seem to have moved. For a moment she wondered if she was seeing things.

The engine stopped and the front door opened. A youngish blonde woman leapt out and bustled round to the back. 'We're not late, are we?' she asked. Marion and Harry stared in astonishment. 'Could you lend a hand?'

The pallbearers glanced up from their huddle to check that no one was speaking to them.

'It's matron,' said Marion. 'I didn't recognise her in black.'

Joyce Keay climbed into the back of the ambulance and lowered the automatic ramp before helping the first of her two passengers to their feet. 'This is Mrs Pocock.'

Harry took the old woman's hands and walked with her slowly down the ramp while Marion unclamped a wheelchair.

'Are you Sheila's son?'

'Her son-in-law.'

Mrs Pocock nodded, leaning against him shyly.

She looked uncomfortable, pressing forward against the edge of the pew with her shoulders slouched and her knees together like a little girl. It was as if she were only just there, one thoughtless gesture and she would simply vanish into the brickwork. One wrong word would be enough to send her stalking back down the aisle. She looked straight ahead, at nothing in particular, and seemed angry. Her puffy, bloodshot eyes were cold.

'Didn't anyone tell you? It's rude to stare.'

Sarah blushed and looked at her feet.

Catherine put her sunglasses back on. 'Come on, for God's sake. Let's get this over with,' she muttered. Jamie sat at the end of the pew like a prison guard. The vicar coughed lightly, once, and handed out orange hymn books.

The coffin came in, balanced precariously on the shoulders of the pallbearers as if it were part of their job to make the carrying look difficult. She can't have weighed more than five stone when she died, thought Marion, flinching as they lowered it on to the table with a bump. She stared at the thickly pleated maroon velvet curtains behind. Towards the end of the service the vicar would press a secret button and the coffin would slide backwards, as if by magic, retreating into a pitch black rectangle. Somewhere on the other side, presumably, were furnaces. But the curtains would swish shut again before the congregation had time to think about that.

A taxi was waiting in the forecourt when they came out of the chapel, dazed and silenced by the brightness of the after-noon, moved almost in spite of themselves by the service. As if, for fifteen minutes, they had actually believed, like theatre-goers, in a character called God and a place called heaven. Now, in the sunshine, they remembered that it had only been a story after all. They clustered in front of the ambulance searching for the right conversation. Marion had not wanted to organise a formal wake so there was nowhere in particular for them to go, and Joyce insisted on returning her patients to St Margaret's straight away.

Catherine trailed out last, avoiding the others. The taxi driver nodded at her and muttered something into his crack-ling radio. With a confusing mixture of regret and relief, Sarah watched as her mother ducked inside, slamming the door shut quietly over her scarf, which dangled out, like a shadow or an oil slick, collapsing into a pile of chiffon on the tarmac below. The engine started and the taxi reversed slowly, dragging it behind. Suddenly Catherine flew forwards into the back of the passenger seat. The taxi's brakes screamed. Sarah ran towards the car but Harry pushed her out of the way and leaned in, groping frantically for the other end of the scarf as Catherine choked and spluttered. 'Don't move,' he commanded, loosening it at last. 'Can you breathe?'

'I think so,' she gasped, slumping back into her seat. Gingerly she lifted a hand to her burning throat. 'Thanks.'

'I'll call a doctor.'

'No don't.'

The driver got out and hurried round to the front of his car, cursing and apologising. Marion and Jamie pointed at the axle. Sarah started to cry. Harry took off his jacket and handed it to his wife. He helped her from the car. A necklace of violent bruises blushed at the base of her throat. 'Come on, let's sit down.' He motioned to a nearby bench and steered her firmly towards it. Catherine took three steps and passed out.

Faraway birds were singing. The warmth of the sun sank blissfully into her black dress. The sharp, sweet smell of cut grass made her think of Saturday afternoons long ago and the picture seemed so vivid that when she opened her eyes she could have wept with disappointment. Harry's anxious face swam into focus.

'You fainted,' he said, gently.

She swallowed and it hurt. Her head was pounding. An inquisitive ant scurried up her shin. She was lying down; the ground was hard. 'What time is it?'

'Nearly four.'

'I'll miss my train.'

'Does it matter?'

Catherine closed her eyes. 'Nothing matters.' She paused. 'Where's Sarah?'

'With Marion and Jamie, over there. I thought you wouldn't want a crowd.'

'I feel as though I'm on my deathbed.' She raised herself onto her elbows and sat up.

'There's no hurry; take your time.'

They drove back from the funeral parlour in convoy, Catherine too shaken to complain. She sat in the front of the battered Rover nursing the torn scarf in her lap, running its two frayed edges between her fingertips, letting the chiffon's minute roughness soothe her nerves. Marion and Jamie led the way, taking a shocked and obedient Sarah with them. Catherine could see her through the distant rear window, a small blonde head. A tractor and trailer loaded with hay pulled out from a side road and the Citroën slowed. They soon caught up with it. Sarah turned round to wave. Harry smiled at her. She mouthed something and pointed to her mother and waved again. Loose straws flew from the tractor, bouncing off their windscreen into the side of the road. A barley field revealed itself through a gap in the hedgerow.

'How far is it?' asked Catherine.

'We're nearly there.'

Marion glanced in the mirror, signalling to overtake. The silhouette of Sarah's head obliterated her view of the metro behind and she inched out cautiously into the right-hand lane, then stepped on the accelerator. As Harry's car shrank away and disappeared, a bolt of pain shot across her gut.

'That load didn't look very secure,' Jamie was saying, in a distant voice. The spasm dulled into a sensation she knew well but hardly dared recognise. There was a second sharp wrench. She threw herself forwards over the steering wheel as the pain expanded and they screamed round a blind corner, swinging out into the oncoming lane. Jamie slid into the door with a jolt. 'Slow down, love.'

Marion's face had gone deathly white, her mouth was twisted with a bitten back howl of pain.

'What's wrong?'

Oh my God, she thought, gritting her teeth as another spasm racked into her, *I'm losing it.*

'You look awful.'

'Thanks.'

'Shall I drive?'

'I can manage,' she gripped the wheel, 'it's not far now.' Inside invisible fingers tore at the lining of her womb.

They screeched into the yard, Jamie opening the door to get out before the car had even stopped.

'Sarah, make a hot water bottle,' he ordered. 'I'm going up with her.'

Marion staggered up the stairs, clutching her stomach in one hand and the bannister with the other. She collapsed on the bed and for a moment the pain seemed to subside.

'Take these.' Jamie handed her three aspirin and a glass of water. 'Shall I call the doctor?'

She shook her head, then stiffened. 'Oh God! Help me to the bathroom. Quick, I'm bleeding.'

Harry walked Catherine straight up to Sarah's room to rest.

She took off her shoes and burrowed between the covers, her teeth chattering.

'How are you feeling?'

'Sick.'

'Warm enough?'

She nodded slightly.

'Is there anything you want?' he said awkwardly.

'A drink.'

In the corridor he bumped into Sarah. 'Marion's ill,' she said importantly, knocking on the door and half walking in. Jamie came over to take the hot water bottle. She stared past him at Marion lying on the bed, curled up, rocking herself, her face and hair shiny with sweat.

'Can I see her?'

'Not yet, love.'

'Is the doctor coming?'

'No.'

She backed out, disappointed.

'What's wrong with her?' asked Harry.

'She's got tummy ache. How's Mum?'

'In shock, I think. Are there any more hot water bottles?'

Marion stared at the cracks in the ceiling. Jamie's hand smoothed her forehead, combing into her damp hair over and over again. In just half an hour this simple gesture had become her clock, her heartbeat. It was as if nothing she couldn't feel existed. There was only pain and relief from pain, her womb and her scalp. Now, though, the contractions were less acute. She remembered the rest of Jamie: his arm, his strong shoulders half-silhouetted against the shining window, his face. She seemed to be waking up. The cracks in the ceiling had been there all along. Her breathing slowed.

'How are you feeling, love?'

'It doesn't hurt so much now.'

'What can I do?'

She blinked and the room snapped into focus; hot tears slid down the sides of her face and into her hair and ears. 'Nothing. It's too late.'

'You can't know—'

'It is.'

'Shh.'

'Don't go.'

'I won't,' he whispered. He closed her eyes with his fingertips.

Catherine lay in her daughter's bed and stared at the wallpaper. Sarah had drawn the blind and turned on the bedside light, which brought a yellow glow to the blue flowery walls. The pillow smelled of her, a mixture of shampoo and the salty, almost acrid, smell of preadolescents. One of her long fine hairs shone on the edge of the duvet like a strand of gold. Catherine moved her head very slowly from side to side, watching the way the light travelled along its arc and back again. The room was quiet.

Sarah knocked gently on the door and shouldered it open without waiting for an answer. 'I've brought you some tea,' she said, resting the cup and saucer on the windowsill.

Catherine allowed her head to be lifted and three pillows slotted in behind. She shuffled herself into a semi-reclined position and waited.

*

It grew dark. The cows stumbled down to the stream. Pink clouds faded into the dusky blue, and Ollie whimpered to be let in. Harry found an onion and some leeks and chopped them up to make soup. The house was very quiet. It felt empty. He opened a bottle of wine and poured two glasses, one for him and one half-full for Sarah. She crept upstairs to see if Marion or Jamie wanted some, pushing open the door just a crack before going in. The last glimmers of daylight fanned across the bed like pale grey shadows. He was lying next to her, above the covers. They didn't move or say a word, so she closed the door quietly and tiptoed back down.

'Why didn't you tell me, love?' he whispered, breaking the silence after Sarah had gone.

Marion looked at him softly, trying to remember. 'I don't know. I should have.' Wasn't that close enough to the truth? She was exhausted. 'I don't know. It felt so right. I just wanted to keep it to myself for a while.' Her look was almost a touch. 'You would have found out soon enough.'

He nodded, running his numb hand through her hair.

'I'm sorry.' She looked at the eiderdown. 'Love, I'm sorry. I should have said. Are you hurt?'

'Yes.' But he was smiling. 'I didn't know you were ready.'

'I'm sorry,' she whispered again.

'That's all right. Tomorrow we'll go and see the doctor. OK?'

'OK.'

'I love you. We'll try again, if we have to. Together.'

'Yes.'

*

Her mother was asleep when Sarah next came in, loaded with sheets. The bedside light still cast its warm yellowy light on the room and sloping, affectionate shadows filled the gaps. Grimacing as its rusty legs scraped the floor, she pulled the spare bed out from the wall and threw off the coverlet.

'What time is it?' Catherine murmured drowsily.

Sarah shrugged. 'After ten? Did I wake you?'

'Mm,' she raised her head, propping it up on her hand to watch as her daughter unfolded a second under-blanket and smoothed it over the mattress meticulously. She spread the sheet. 'Who's that for?' she asked.

'You, of course,' said Sarah, making a hospital corner and lifting the mattress to tuck it beneath.

'Aren't you strong.'

'Am I?' She lifted the second corner, proudly.

Catherine took a long, deep breath. 'What shampoo do you use?' she asked.

Sarah looked up in surprise. 'Same as you, of course.'

'Really? That's odd . . .' Catherine stretched her feet, pointing and relaxing the toes as if to get her circulation going again. She didn't want to change beds. She wanted to stay where she was.

'Why don't you sleep in that bed, I'll stay here,' she suggested, almost imperiously.

'But I'm making it up for you,' answered Sarah. The sheet was completely tucked in now, and the surface of the bed was as smooth and white as a china plate.

It looks cold, thought Catherine. 'Can't I stay in your bed?'

Sarah stopped stuffing the pillowcase and examined her mother's pale, creased face, the shadows under her eyes, the blotchy tear-stained nose. Somehow her expression seemed brighter, petulant almost.

'If you like.' She shook the pillowcase and plumped it, then dropped it at the head of the bed; the fresh sheet wrinkled. 'Anything you like.'

I have taken the saucepan off the heat. Once the temperature has reached soft ball you are supposed to leave it to cool, beating every now and then to test the consistency, the idea being to catch it just as it first begins to thicken. Sticky brown chocolate bubbles rise to the surface and disappear. This is the part I always get wrong. When Mum sees what a pig's ear I have made of it she will crow, and I will tell her, piously, that it's the taste that counts and she will roll her eyes, pantomiming.

'After everything I have taught you, how can you still be so naïve?' she'll say, pulling rank.

'Mum.' I fold myself round her bedroom door, peering into the dark. 'I'm going now.'

'Goodbye then,' she says, curtly. She has taken off her minidress and crawled under the covers, though how she can possibly be cold on a day like this I fail to understand. She sniffs; she has been crying. White tissue-flowers litter the bed.

'Unless you want to have some cake now?' I offer.

'No.'

'OK. Well. Goodbye.'

'Goodbye.'

'I'll phone you later.' When I was a child I used to listen very carefully to what she said, trying to find a way through her blackness. I think I listened too carefully and, without necessarily meaning to, forgave her everything. Back then I understood what love was, what it is to lose it. I was pro-euthanasia.

I close the door and walk downstairs. Someone has crammed a fistful of taxi flyers through the letterbox. David is probably home by now, gingerly stepping down to his front door, one hand pressed against the wall for balance. The earth seems to tilt, shrinking away from his feet with every step. His shoes are ocean-liners, the impenetrable mosses at the edge of the garden path an archipelago. Maybe she's right, maybe he knew she wouldn't say yes. If anything were to happen to him, I wonder, how long would it be before the neighbours noticed?

There is a message waiting for me back at the flat. I rewind the tape and press play. Suddenly the room is flooded with the sound of Ben's voice.

'Hi, love,' he says. 'Oh, I forgot you're at your mother's. Never mind. Just to say I've arrived safe and sound and every-one here sends you their love. God it was hot on the motorway! I'm about to go and jump in the sea, it's high tide. Anyway, see you Sunday. Lots of love.'

He wanted me to meet his family and, last year, took me to Cornwall for a weekend in September – according to the almanac, the weekend of the biggest tides of the century. We drove south along the coast so he could show me where the beaches normally were. The bridge across the estuary in

Bideford had to be closed to traffic. Lying awake that night, alone, in the guest room, I thought of all that water slipping back into the Atlantic. I thought of thunder storms and other, physical things I still don't understand.

The next day had been sunny and warm and we went to a secret cove to catch lobster. The sea had already rolled a long way back and there were still two hours to go before low tide. Sharp rocks jutted up innocently from a bed of sand. We took off our shoes and walked towards the horizon. Ben showed me how to knock off limpets with the metal of the lobster hook – a sharp sideways blow when they're least expecting it – which you drop into the rock pools as a lure. Apparently it's possible to catch a lobster even without the limpet, using barbed wire.

Rock by rock we clambered further and further out, cutting our feet on barnacles and chucking limpets into the water more, now, as food than bait since we still hadn't seen one and our hearts weren't really in the mood for killing. Gradually the pools grew wider and deeper, sandy-bottomed and clear of seaweed, good enough to swim in. We took off our clothes and waded through. Overhead the gulls were in a frenzy. The sea was calm, and so far away you couldn't even hear what it said.

I rewind the tape again, picturing him in the water, and press erase. A wave slides in, glittering and clear at the top like glass. You can see fish in it. Foam curls over as it bears down on him and he dives for safety. It breaks, the sea goes flat and quiet, silver in the late afternoon sun. Just as I am about to panic, Ben resurfaces, laughing and whooping, shaking the icy water from his hair. He swims a few strokes further out and rolls over, gazing back at the land. I have never known anyone so capable of happiness. I pick up the phone.

'Mum, it's me. I'm sorry I left so abruptly,' I begin. 'Are you OK?'